The
Messenger

The Messenger

A NOVEL

Mayra Montero

TRANSLATED FROM THE SPANISH
BY EDITH GROSSMAN

Perennial

An Imprint of HarperCollinsPublishers

All chapter titles are taken from the libretto of Giuseppe Verdi's *Aïda*.

A hardcover edition of this book was published by HarperFlamingo, an imprint of HarperCollins Publishers, in 1999.

HarperCollins books may be purchased for educational, business, or sales promotional use. For information please write: Special Markets Department, HarperCollins Publishers Inc., 10 East 53rd Street, New York, NY 10022.

First Perennial edition published 2000.

Designed by Kris Tobiassen

The Library of Congress has catalogued the hardcover edition as follows:

Montero, Mayra, 1952–
    [Como un mensajero tuyo. English]
    The Messenger : a novel / Mayra Montero
      p. cm.
    ISBN: 0-06-019223-2
    1. Caruso, Enrico, 1873–1921—Fiction.   I. Title.
  PQ7440.M56C6613   1999
  863—dc21   98-41176

ISBN 0-06-092961-8 (pbk.)

00 01 02 03 04 ❖/HHD 10 9 8 7 6 5 4 3 2 1

In gratitude to Vivian Martínez and Mario Flores,
for their long hours in the newspaper archives of Havana

In memory of Enriqueta Cheng,
from someone who always believed her

Brucio sul colle spazio e tempo,
Come un tuo messaggero,
Come il sogno, divina morte.

—GIUSEPPE UNGARETTI

Il Messagger s'avanzi!

*C*alle Amargura," he told the cabdriver, and then hesitated for a moment: Amargura 73 . . . Amargura 78 . . . ? He looked for the paper in his pocket: "Calle Amargura 75," he added. Street of Bitterness, he said to himself, and with the bitter thought came the premonition that perhaps the old woman had died.

"Suppose she's dead?" he murmured, clutching at the packet of photographs. The driver looked at him in the rearview mirror.

"What did you say?"

He shook his head and was careful not to speak again. He felt ill at ease whenever he was in this section of Old Havana— repelled by the stench of black water mixed with the stink of spent diesel fuel, appalled by the balconies propped up by rotting timbers propped up in turn by other timbers on the verge of rotting. Occasionally a balcony collapsed, leaving behind blank windows and the raw-looking spine of a staircase.

"This is it. Amargura 75," said the driver.

When he got out, he searched the door for a clue: black crepe, a sealed lock, a sign saying the house was for sale. Then he remembered that in Havana nobody put up crepe or For Sale signs anymore, and not even the houses of people who died without heirs were sold. In any case, another family, maybe two, would soon occupy it. The house could easily be divided in three, he thought, and he knocked at the door.

A minute, a minute and a half, went by. A woman crossed the street, stared at him and then glanced at the closed door. He was tempted to ask if she knew whether Señora Enriqueta was at home. For a moment he imagined her reply: "Didn't anyone tell you? The old lady died a month ago."

"She's dead," he whispered, and then he heard the sound of footsteps. The door opened; he felt dark air on his face, and a shadow said:

"Welcome."

"A promise is a promise," he exclaimed, holding the packet up for the old woman to see.

She moved aside. A smell reached him from the interior of the house, the stink of damp rags, cat urine, and rotting potatoes. Once, in one of the rooms, he had seen a heap of potatoes piled against the wall; some were inedible, sprouting long tentacles that twined along the caned back of a sofa.

"When did you arrive?" she asked.

"Yesterday," he said, "but since I can't call you . . ."

She sighed. "Four years, two months, twenty-something days I've been without a phone. Why can't they fix a phone?"

They walked down the unlit hallway toward the dining room. She led the way, dragging her feet and giving off her own distinctive smell: menthol, dissolved pills, a mix of perpetual sweat and rancid vanilla. As they passed the kitchen, he caught a glimpse of the cat.

"Canio," she called, and patted it on the head. "He's sick," said the old woman. "He hardly eats."

They sat at the table; he opened the packet and took out some photographs. He also brought out a second package wrapped in gift paper.

"You didn't ask me for this, but I know you'll like it."

She put it to one side, not looking at it, and held out her hand for the photographs.

"On the back of each one," he said, giving her the first picture, "I've written the date and the place where I took it. This,

for example, is Via San Giovannello. San Giovannello 7—
that's where he was born."

She adjusted her glasses, looked at the photo briefly, then
read the line on the back.

"Via San Giovannello . . . ," she repeated.

"This is the hotel," he said, handing her another photograph. "Look at the name, Vesuvio, and the corner I marked in
red ink. That's where the room is. That's where he died."

She placed this photograph on top of the first and took the
third one.

"His grave," he murmured. "I have two others, but this is the
best shot. Do you see the stone? . . . August 2, 1921. Those are
the flowers I brought him in your name."

He thought she turned pale, or perhaps she had been pale
from the beginning, from the moment she opened the door and
realized he had come to claim his part of the bargain. When she
finished with the third photograph, he showed her a small
album.

"The pictures from La Galleria are all here: a total of fifty-
two. I took pictures of the buildings, the shops. . . . This one, for
instance, is a record store. And the roof is there too: you wanted
to see that roof, didn't you? And these are of the pavement; it's
still the original one, the same one where he walked."

They were silent as she looked through the album. He felt
that he ought to leave her alone, and he got up without making
noise, walked down the hall, and stopped at the kitchen. He
called Canio two or three times, but the cat had disappeared.
When he went back to the dining room, the old woman had
closed the album and was slowly opening the package wrapped
in gift paper.

"It's just a memento of La Scala," he said quickly.

She took out what seemed to be a small picture, ran her finger around the frame, and then gently touched the engraved metal plate gleaming in the center.

"If you'd like, I'll hang it for you. Just tell me where."

The old woman did not answer. She collected the photographs, stood up from the table, and walked slowly toward the sideboard.

"I'll look at them later, when I can take my time. Would you like some water?"

"I'm leaving tomorrow," he said. "You already know what I'd like."

He was prepared for the worst. For her to say that she thought he wasn't coming back and had sold it; or that it had been stolen one night—recently there had been a lot of stealing in the city; or that she had thought it over and changed her mind. Nobody could force her to part with her only treasure.

"I'd just like to know," the old woman said, "if you're going to keep it."

He shook his head.

"I've arranged to sell it. For less money than I expected. What's valuable is the gold, because nobody believes the story: you and I know it's true, but there's no way to prove it."

She stood, motionless, her hands resting on the back of a chair.

"Who did you sell it to, if you don't mind my asking?"

"A collector. Somebody who wants very much to believe us and who won't melt it down or sell it later."

"That's the least of it," she replied. "Sometimes I think the best thing would have been to throw it into the ocean."

"You can't do that now. I promised I'd bring those photographs, leave flowers on his grave, walk the entire length of La Galleria. You know, La Galleria looks like a street in Tokyo. Always full of Japanese . . ."

He heard her laugh. For a woman her age she had a young laugh, like a distant bell, which did not seem to come from that ruined mouth.

"You can't throw it into the ocean," he continued. "A bargain is a bargain, and I've done my part."

She went back to the sideboard, hesitated for a few seconds, and finally pulled open a drawer. She took out a ball of newspaper and placed it on the table.

"Here it is."

He picked it up and with some impatience began to unwrap it, tossing the paper to the floor, expecting at any moment to see a gleam, an edge. At last he uncovered a rough nugget of gold, about the size of an egg.

"Read it again," she told him.

He turned it around to the tiny plaque:

IN MEMORIA DELLA BOMBA
CHE CI HA FATTO ARDERE

Next to the plaque, embedded in the gold, was a sliver of wood.

"That's a piece of wood from the wreckage."

"I know," he said. "I'll tell the buyer."

"If you prefer," she went on, "I can give you those details in writing. When my mother was alive, the two of us wrote down what happened. And I interviewed a few people."

She moved away, not waiting for an answer, and he picked up the paper from the floor. He tried to wrap the nugget again, but one of the sheets ripped between his fingers, and then he fitted together the torn pieces and read the headline: 29 YEARS SINCE BOMBING OF TEATRO NACIONAL. WAITER A SUSPECT, BUT CASE NEVER SOLVED.

He checked the date of the newspaper: June 13, 1949.

The old woman returned with a sheaf of papers tied with blue ribbon. On the first page, in block letters, was written: THE STORY OF AIDA PETRIRENA CHENG, AS TOLD TO HER DAUGHTER, ENRIQUETA CHENG.

"If the buyer is a collector, he'll want to know what happened."

"Absolutely," he said. "Don't you want to keep this newspaper?"

He showed her the headline, and she shook her head.

"I don't want to keep anything."

He finished rewrapping the nugget and put it in the bag where he had carried the photographs.

"I know there's not enough money in the world to pay for this," he said, offering her an envelope. She extended her hand in a gesture of refusal, but he got to his feet and placed the envelope on the sideboard. "It's dollars. You'll have to buy Canio a little food; those bones are killing him."

"He can't hunt anything," she admitted. "If I let him out, they'll catch him and boil him. Do you know that people eat cats boiled?"

He put an arm around her shoulders and lied, looking into her eyes:

"I'll be back next year. I'll come and see you."

"We may not be here. I may have to eat Canio myself."

He pretended not to hear and picked up the papers on the table.

"May I read this too?"

"It would be a good idea if you did," she replied, "though it may bore you. When my mother decided to tell me everything, I spent hours writing down what she said. I can't write anymore; I can't even read."

She walked with him to the door, and they both stopped to look at the cat, who managed a sorrowful meow.

"Canio's saying goodbye," she whispered.

They went to the entrance, and he looked up at the balconies.

"Amargura isn't a good name for a street."

"Of course it isn't," she said, "but you must understand, it doesn't matter anymore."

*T*his is the story of my mother. A story that begins on the Feast of the Wise Men in the year 1920, when she was a twenty-seven-year-old widow who had lost her firstborn child.

My mother's name was Aida Petrirena Cheng—I have the same last name—and she was the daughter of Noro Cheng Po, a Chinese immigrant who set up a business in Cuba, and Domitila Cuervo, a mulatta who was a love child, too. Domitila's mother, a black Lucumi woman, was named Petrona, and her father was a Spaniard whose first name we never found out, though we did know his family name: that was the Cuervo with which he recognized his daughter.

My mother told me her story when she learned she was sick. At first we didn't plan to write it down, but as time passed I found it very difficult to remember all the names and dates. And so I asked her to speak slowly, I bought some notebooks, and I began to write everything she said.

We began on March 5, 1952, the day I turned thirty-one, and finished eight months later, on November 16.

That night, just at nine o'clock, we both wrote the words "The End."

La sacra Iside consultasti?...

ive months before the bomb exploded, my godfather received into his hands the song that would break my life in two.

That happened in January in the year 1920. I went with my mother to visit him—we always went to see him on the Feast of the Wise Men—and besides giving me my present, a little gold medal, he said to me:

"Sit down, I'm going to look into you."

Looking into me meant looking into my future, and he asked my mother to wait outside. My godfather was named José de Calazán Bangoché, he was already an old man when I knew him but he grew even older afterward, and he kept on growing old like the trunk of a tree and didn't die till I was forty-two, that's how old I was when I went to his funeral.

On that day in 1920 we went into the room where he kept his altar and he rubbed my forehead with some pieces of coconut and something I thought was lard; he told me to show him the palms of my hands and he spit into them, then he rubbed the spit with his finger and put that finger over my lips. We sat on the floor face-to-face, and between us was the old straw mat with black drawings. He leaned his back against the wall and began to rub the *ékuele*—that's a chain made of eight sections: eight pieces that sometimes are coconut and sometimes turtle shell. While he rubbed the *ékuele* he prayed to his saints, he blessed his dead and called for them: his dead godfather, his godfather's godfather, and all the great *babalawos* who had passed the power down to him.

"Ifá says . . . ," he whispered, and threw the chain, and it twisted on the mat as if it had a life of its own. He picked it up and threw it again, and he did the same thing a few times. Each time he threw it hurt him, the vein in his neck would swell and he would moan his prayers, at first it sounded like he was retching. After a while he grew calm and took my right hand, raised it to his mouth, and talked into my hand. I felt his hot breath between my fingers, a breath so hard it was like he was vomiting up a bird, a crazed creature trying to escape.

"Ifá says a man will come," said my godfather. "He will come to crown you and tell you that you are the queen of his thoughts. Before that you will hear the thunder, the walls will fall down, there will be dust and fire. On that day—listen carefully—take your protection out of your clothing and put it over your hair. Then you bring me that man, you will have to bring him to me." He picked up the *ékuele* and hid it between his hands. "He is coming to die. But if you don't want that, if you bring him to me right away, he will not die. Bring him so you won't be tainted. He is not coming to die: he is already dead when he comes."

I remember I felt a chill run down my spine and I screamed a scream that wasn't mine but like the scream of an animal, a poisoned dog that had control of my throat. My godfather shook me and slapped my face, and I fell back and fainted. When I came to, my mother was holding my head, I was naked from the waist up because my blouse tore when I went into the trance, and José de Calazán was kneeling beside me, asking me to drink a tea he had brewed. While I drank I looked into his eyes and remembered what he had said, and that was like remembering what was going to happen: first the noise and then the wreckage, and the face of a man, his whole body, coming out of the smoke.

"He's white," I shouted. "Didn't you see that he was white?"

My godfather shrugged. My mother began to straighten my skirt, and then she smoothed my hair with her fingers. And wiped my face with a handkerchief.

"I wish there was a way to stop him," she whispered, "stop him on the ocean so he doesn't come to Cuba."

My godfather shook his head.

"He is coming to die but it's better if he doesn't. That's the only thing we can stop. Stop him from dying with your daughter, let him drop his burden somewhere else. He is coming with a burden, rotting away while he lives. Ay, ay, ay, my head hurts."

José de Calazán shook his whole body and covered his ears. My mother seemed very frightened and asked me to wait outside. I never knew what she talked about to Calazán, I only know she came out of that house with her head bowed and her eyes full of tears, and without looking at me she stretched out her hand: because of that hand I knew she was afraid. My godfather lived in the village of Regla, on the other side of the bay, and there was a launch that carried us back and forth. On the launch that took us back to Havana, my mother threw seven pennies into the water and gave me another seven so that I could throw them in.

"Your godfather wants you to take baths in the ocean and rinse your head with indigo. And do that every Friday until we have to go back."

She said this so I would know that when we went back, it would have to be with that man.

"He heard music in the *ékuele*," my mother went on, "music that said your name. He told me it's very strange because the *ékuele* never sings."

I asked which name, because I always had two: Aida, which is what she wanted to call me, and Petrirena, the name she had to give me because my grandmother asked her to. My father wanted me to have a different name, maybe a Chinese one, but my mother refused. From Noro Cheng, that was his name, I got my eyes and hair, and that's why people called me "Chinita." My mother didn't like it when they called me "Chinita," she always became very offended and said her daughter's name was Aida. Then she would comfort me—I think she was comforting herself—telling me that as time passed, people would call me by my right name. But time passed and it got worse, and we both became resigned, or pretended we were resigned: my Chinese part was the first thing people saw.

My mother was a slim mulatta who always moved very fast and hardly made any noise when she walked. My grandmother, my mother's mother, was a heavy, noisy black woman who couldn't take two steps without bumping into the furniture. I remember the sound of her voice, it was very loud and she had a hoarse laugh like a man's. This grandmother lived with us for a while but I didn't know her very well because she died when I was little. But what I remember most about her was that the whites of her eyes were yellow. I always looked at her eyes and then I'd look in the mirror, trying to see if one day mine would be like hers. My grandmother said I didn't have to worry, hers had turned yellow because her mother was Lucumi and her father, my great-grandfather, was Mandinga, and that combination always produced bad-tempered children with bulging eyes that slowly changed color.

I don't think my mother ever loved Noro Cheng, her husband. She met him when he was already pretty old and she was only sixteen. Since her own mother had so many children, and there was no trace of her father, as soon as the Chinaman offered to take her they gave her to him with only the clothes on her back. A Chinaman, my mother would say, was the worst man a woman could marry but all a girl like her could hope for, since she was poor and had nappy hair. In the beginning the Chinaman hardly talked to her, and the few times he did, my mother could hardly understand him. After a couple of years, when she thought her husband was just too old to make any babies, her belly swelled up and I came into the world. Or at least that's the story they told me for a long time. Then my father got sick and my mother took his place in a little laundry he had with two other paisanos, two Chinamen. I stayed home with my father, and that's how I started to talk to him in Cantonese and how my mother got used to hearing us talk without understanding us. She would come home tired after ironing so many clothes and fall asleep to the sound of our voices. She didn't talk to us much, and she didn't kiss us either. My family never was a family that kissed.

When I was little I was very attached to my father. I didn't care that he was a Chinaman, or would spit against the walls, or smelled the way they all smell: like some vegetable they eat. When he died one morning in December, after coughing for so many days, more and more Chinamen started to come to the house and asked my mother to let them watch over his body in their own way, with singing and incense. My mother said yes, and they were the ones who took him to the cemetery the next day and buried him the way they buried all their paisanos: with his head pointing to the sunrise. My mother went on working at the laundry, and I think at some point she became involved with another Chinaman, one of the men who picked up and delivered the clothes. They never lived together, but people talked, and when I got bigger and started to work there, too, I felt ashamed. This was when I began to turn away from my mother, from that laundry where the Chinamen would take off their shirts and eat their noodles and sometimes drop dead of the heat. Then I persuaded my mother to sell her share—it wasn't very much money but enough for us to buy a sewing machine, in those days that was a real luxury: a luxury that would earn us some money.

That's how our business started: my mother was a very good seamstress, and she taught me how to sew. After a while, white ladies began to come to us for their dresses. One of them was a teacher named Ester, a very refined woman who started to go gray very young. She seemed much older than me, but there was only a difference of six or seven years between us. One afternoon Ester asked her husband to pick up some sewing for her. Baldomero Socada talked to me for a long time, until it was dark, and then my mother, who had a good nose for tragedies, asked him if he didn't think it was time he took the clothes home to his wife. Baldomero left but came back the next day and asked me to sew a shirt for him. The day he came for his fitting, I was fascinated and couldn't stop looking at the blond hair on his chest. That was the start of a life, a daughter was born from that look, and it was no accident she turned out so mixed: sort of blond but with nappy hair and eyes that were green and then suddenly looked Chinese, and even some Mandinga way in the back.

A little while before this girl was born, Baldomero moved in with us. All he brought from his old life was a picture of his dead Ester, who was so refined she took poison when she found out her husband was going to have a child with another woman, a mulatta seamstress, and, to make matters even worse, someone they called "Chinita."

Her taking poison always tormented me because my mother and José de Calazán had both warned me it was very bad if someone died thinking about a person ready to be born. And so with that shadow, that rancor hanging over her, I gave birth to a little girl we called Esperanza. Baldomero gave her his name, Socada; he had never been able to give it to anybody before because he didn't have children with Ester.

Our daughter grew up seeing that photograph hanging on the dining room wall. Gray-haired and sweet in life, Ester changed after she died. If Esperanza glanced at her at night, in the morning she woke up with a fever. That must be why my mother got into the habit of sprinkling the picture; she sprinkled it with holy water, and that made things even worse because with all those drops rolling down her face, it looked like Ester's photograph was crying. Baldomero wouldn't look at it, but our daughter—she was always a strange little girl—she would go over to it and stare and stare, like there was some kind of contest between them.

Baldomero died suddenly, on the street, on Esperanza's fifth birthday. I was twenty-four, and it didn't seem to me I had lost a husband, it was as though I'd given back something that wasn't mine. Before long the little girl followed him. I couldn't look at Ester's picture anymore because as soon as Baldomero died we took it down, put it in the coffin, and buried it with him. But Esperanza kept turning her eyes to the empty spot on the wall, and then she wouldn't move, she would whisper a conversation, we couldn't understand her words but what she was doing worried us. And then one morning she woke up with a fever, and instead of getting better the way she always did she had convulsions, and we lost her that same night. My mother thought I'd go out of my mind, but the months went by and I went on sewing, and when she had been dead for a year I visited her grave and brought her a little dress, and visited Baldomero's grave and brought him a shirt. The two offerings were simple, but they brought me peace.

A peace that was troubled in 1920, when my godfather

heard the song that said my name in the *ékuele*. My mother remembered that Ester played the piano and sang a little, but I remembered something more serious: I remembered that it had been nine years ago, on the Feast of the Wise Men, when Ester found out about me and Baldomero and the child who was on the way. That same night she poured the poison—it was rat poison—into her café con leche.

"José de Calazán heard thunder too," I told my mother. "We'll have to wait till May."

She began to prepare an *omiero*, a potion to purify the house. When it was finished she said a few prayers, and for the first time in years I heard her say some phrases in the old language, the Lucumí language that my grandmother taught her.

"I'll go back to see your godfather," she said suddenly. "Maybe we have to get that picture. Maybe Ester doesn't want her photograph mixed up with Baldomero's bones."

"Maybe," was all I said.

"I'll get it out if we have to get it," she said, showing a lot of courage. "You let me know when that demon shows up."

Il mistero fatal . . .

That May there was a lot of lightning. The thunder was so loud it shook the walls, and there were little claps of thunder far away, like the footsteps of a devil walking round us.

My mother went to see José de Calazán, and I went with her to Regla. I waited for her outside the house, but through the open door I could hear their voices, the whispers of the *baba-lawo*, the sound of her crying. In their conversation they used some phrases in the Lucumi language, phrases that Calazán saved for difficult moments. Then they raised their voices and their talk grew stronger, their shouts grew louder, until they became tired, or their words turned into stones. Finally, they spit out those stones and lit cigars.

In the little boat that took us back to Havana, my mother said that my godfather had forbidden her to take Ester's picture out of the grave where it was buried along with Baldomero's bones. You couldn't give bones air, or light, or grief, and we wouldn't fix anything by troubling them. I felt relieved because I didn't like the idea of opening the coffin of a man I had once known as strong and blond, and finding only his bones, I didn't even know what color they would be. And I didn't feel brave enough to look at Ester's picture, at her face come back from dust and darkness, her expression after so many years. That made me afraid.

My mother said that in cases like mine, you had to turn to the power of the paisanos. She called all the Chinese paisanos, those who had been my father's friends and those who hadn't. One of the paisanos was Yuan Pei Fu, who used to sell fruit and in his old age devoted himself to cultivating his power: the power of the blacks mixed with the power of the dragons. The result of those two powers was a warrior surrounded by smoke: Sanfancón.

"Calazán can't do any more," my mother repeated. And what the black *nganga* can't do, the Chinese *nganga* always can.

Yuan Pei Fu lived in a house on Calle Manrique, just before Real de la Zanja, in the heart of Chinatown. Seven of his paisanos lived there with him, and my mother knew them all. Those Chinamen wouldn't look us in the eye, they mumbled when they talked or didn't talk at all, but they treated my mother like one of the family. There weren't any women in the house, and she acted as though it was hers: as soon as she walked in she began to straighten and clean, she would pick up the clothes and wash the dishes, change the sheets and hang up the clean towels she brought once a week because the China-men didn't own any; I wondered what they used before to dry their hands.

When I was a little girl, my father used to take me there too. He'd stay in one of the rooms, smoking, and I'd wander around looking at the Chinese lanterns. Yuan Pei Fu, who was the Great Olúo, the *babalawo*, the head brujo, would give me candies, and there was another Chinaman, a cripple, who cut little dolls out of paper and gave them to me to play with. When I turned fifteen, I had to bring an offering to Sanfancón, who was master of the sword and the thunder. To tell me the story of this saint, whose real name was Cuang Cong and who had lost his head in battle, Yuan Pei Fu would raise his arms and run around the house shouting "My head! Where's my head?" Then he would squat beside me and tell me the sad part of the story that began on the Ship of Death, during the Twelfth Moon in the forty-seventh year of the Emperor Tu Kong. The ship was the frigate *Oquendo*, and the date of moons and emperors was January 2, 1847. The day when more than three hundred Chinese left Canton to come to work in Cuba. Yuan Pei Fu was eight years old then, and he traveled with his father, who was the guardian of an image of Cuang Cong. At night the men would gather around the image, burn incense, and ask the saint to let them reach land safely. But that didn't happen, because a few days after they set sail the sickness broke out, cholera or typhus, and the men died on deck, gasping for breath and flopping around like little fish. They had to throw ninety-six bodies into the ocean, and Yuan Pei Fu's father was one of them, but before he died he told his son to take care of the image of Cuang Cong. After that, Yuan Pei Fu never let it out of his sight again, and he carried it off the ship when they landed in the village of Regla. José de Calazán, my godfather, hadn't been born yet, but his father, Moro Calazán, was in the crowd that came down to the docks to watch them walk off the ship. At first the people laughed: it was the first time they had seen Chinese slaves chained up like blacks, but even more ragged and desperate, with sunken eyes and their feet swollen with seawater. In the middle of all those men was a child, a little boy carrying an image that looked like Changó to the people of the Lucumi nation.

The saints are the same everywhere, they're the same in China and in Guinea. That's what José de Calazán and Yuan Pei Fu decided on the day my mother brought them together so they could talk. They met in Regla, in Calazán's house, and it was really an event because the Chinese *babalawos* never met with the black *babalawos*. They drank their drinks, they talked about their *orishas*, and Calazán said it was a great coincidence that the scared little Chinese boy his father had seen walking off a boat had turned into such a wise and clever old man.

My mother said that for this reason, and for other reasons I didn't know and couldn't even imagine, my godfather, José de Calazán, would not be offended if we asked Yuan Pei Fu for help.

"The saints," my mother said, "are blood brothers. So are the *babalawos*. And you have the blood of a paisano."

She didn't mention it again, not even on the morning when she woke me just before dawn and told me to get dressed because we both had to pay a visit. We left Amargura and went straight to Calle Manrique. My mother was talking to herself, walking fast and looking down at the ground, and I thought she was practicing what she would say to Yuan Pei Fu. When we came to the Chinamen's house she crossed herself, took out her key, knocked twice, hard, the way she always did, and opened the door. It was dark inside, but my mother knew all the corners and rooms where the paisanos slept, two to a room except for Yuan Pei Fu, who had his own room and altar, and the cripple, who slept in the middle of the living room. At that hour most of the Chinamen were out, selling what they sold: the dried peaches they called "ears," little figures made of sesame seeds or roasted peanuts, and a fish that had black flesh whether it was fresh or salted, a disgusting thing that I didn't think was used for anything good.

My mother went straight to Yuan Pei Fu's room, pushed open the door without knocking, and pulled me in by the arm. The Chinaman was squatting in a corner, smoking or burning sticks of incense. You could hardly see anything there was so much smoke. Only the image of Sanfancón, above us, guarded by a circle of thick candles.

"The man is in Cuba," Yuan Pei Fu announced, his voice coming from a distant place, not his mouth or throat but somewhere up high, from the mist or the clear blue sky. "I've been seeing him for days."

I wanted to ask who he was talking about, who was the man who had come to us and how did he see him, but my mother fell to her knees, raised her hands to her face, and looked as if she would burst into tears.

"He's very close," the Chinaman added, and then he went on talking in Cantonese. My mother raised her head and began to drink in those words, as if she understood them all. Yuan Pei Fu didn't say goodbye to me that day, he couldn't even smile or smooth my hair, which was his way of telling me goodbye. We left him sunk in that pit of mysteries, shaping strange figures with his hands, joining and twisting those slender fingers of his—in the dark they looked like worms to me.

Before we went back home, my mother wanted to go to the Church of La Merced and make an offering to Santa Flora, the beheaded saint we always prayed to. We bought white flowers, lit a candle, and kneeled in front of the golden goblet that held the tongue of the virgin saint. My mother crossed herself and made the sign of the cross over me with holy water, bent her head and prayed, and after that prayer she seemed more peaceful. When we were back home we didn't talk about Yuan Pei Fu again, or the few words he had said to us.

The month of May ended quietly. Nothing unusual happened in my life, and when June started I felt relieved. My mother noticed this and warned me not to forget what Calazán had said, to keep it in mind no matter how much time went by.

One Sunday after lunch, I got ready to deliver some sewing we had finished on Saturday. Two of the parcels were going to the same house on Calle Compostela. The third had to go a little farther: to the Hotel Inglaterra. Of all the things that happened that day, the saddest was my mother's face when we said goodbye. She'd had a premonition and said she was thinking about my grandmother, who had come to her in a dream and talked to her from the other world in the Lucumi language. But the thing she had noticed most was that the whites of her eyes, which had always been yellow, had turned white again. My mother saw the change as a sign. We hugged and I went out. I delivered the first two packages without any problem, and sometime after four I walked down Paseo del Prado, turned onto Calle San Miguel, and pushed opened the little metal door to the kitchen of the Hotel Inglaterra. The cook was glad to see me; I gave her the package of clothes, and she paid me. Then she asked if I'd like something to drink, and though my mother and I usually didn't spend time chatting with our clients, I felt thirsty that afternoon and said I would. Two men were also working in the kitchen: one was washing pans and the other was peeling vegetables. The cook gave me a glass of lemonade in a pretty blue glass, but I hardly had time to raise it to my mouth when we heard a huge explosion. She shouted "Holy God!" and looked at the men, who ran outside to the street. I dropped the glass and took out my protection, a little bag that Calazán had strengthened for just this moment. I tied it to my hair and waited.

"It came from the theater," one of the men shouted. "The ceiling collapsed, a lot of people must be hurt."

I tried to leave, but the cook held on to me. She said I'd be safe there, the streets were full of commotion and screaming, and there might even be more explosions. I stepped back and leaned against the table where one of the men had just been chopping squash. I picked up a stringy clump of seeds, squeezed them, closed my eyes, and then it seemed I could hear the voice of Yuan Pei Fu:

"He's very close." I opened my eyes again and looked toward the street, toward the open door, and at that moment a man appeared in the doorway. Again the cook exclaimed "Holy

God," and I began to whisper the litany my godfather had told me to say: "*Iyá nlá, Iyá Oyibó, Iyá erú, Iyá, mi lánu . . .* ," that's a prayer that means: "Great Mother, Mother of the whites, Mother of the blacks, have mercy."

The man rushed in, tore off his cloak, and dropped it on the vegetable skins scattered around the floor. All he wore under the cloak was a white tunic, and in that tunic he looked to me like a king from another time, a warrior *orisha* running from the fury of another *orisha*. I wanted to run too, but I had lost my voice and my will and was thinking that my fate was sealed: the man who had come to crown me, the man who had come to die in Cuba, or who was dead already, marked and condemned by the saint in his own head, had come out of the smoke and the noise and finally stood trembling before me.

"Bring me a glass of water."

He said it with authority, and the cook hurried to give it to him. He looked around for somewhere to sit and found a stool beside me. He came toward me slowly, passing his hand across his forehead. On his head he still wore something that looked like a turban decorated with snakes, then he took it off and put it on the table next to the chopped squash. I could smell the odor of his clothes, I saw his sandals and his feet covered with soot: I think I began to love him because of the tips of those small toes that seemed like women's toes to me. Many days later, when we were far from Havana, I caressed those toes and confessed in a whisper that it had all started there, in the place where the Chinese *babalawos* say you can find the tail of the soul. He began to laugh and swore he could hardly remember anything about that afternoon: the explosion, the dust that had gone up his nose and down his throat, the horror he had felt because his throat was sacred. He couldn't even remember that the cook brought him a glass of water, and that before she gave it to him she recognized him and stepped back in a kind of daze: "Excuse me, Señor," she kept repeating, then finally she reacted and handed him the glass.

He drank the water and was quiet and thoughtful for a while, but suddenly he asked where he was. The cook told him he was in the kitchen of the Hotel Inglaterra, and he said he couldn't go back to his hotel, the Sevilla, and it would be better for him to stay in this one. He asked if the Inglaterra was safe, and that's when I remembered my godfather. I had the feeling that José de Calazán was standing beside me, whispering into my ear what I had to do, telling me that if I wanted to, if I took him away, the man wouldn't die.

"The Inglaterra isn't safe," I lied, "but I can take you to a place that is."

The cook looked at me as if she couldn't believe what she'd just heard, she stammered a few words that didn't change anything because he stood up right away and said: "Let's go." Then she took me by the arm. She was a good friend of my mother's and knew very well who José de Calazán was, that's why I told her I was going him to take him to my godfather, that Calazán himself had told me to do that. Nobody argued with Calazán's orders, least of all a woman, and so she didn't argue, but she was so bewildered she dug her nails into my arm. Her nails were short, but she had strong fingers.

"Aida, do you know who this man is?"

I knew and didn't know. He was Calazán's nightmare. And mine.

"Girl, that's Caruso!" And she pulled her hand away as if it had been burned.

*E*nrico Caruso landed in Havana on May 5, 1920, suffering from toothache and wishing he could turn around and sail straight back to New York. He was forty-seven years old, a victim of chronic migraine, who smoked a minimum of fifty cigarettes a day and woke each morning of his life with shooting pains in his liver and the taste of gall in his mouth.

When he demanded ten thousand dollars a performance from the impresario who proposed that he sing in Cuba, he was certain the man would tell him it was impossible. That was a lunatic figure, an outrageous fee, more than he had ever been paid in any other city in the world and more than any other tenor would even have dreamed of earning. But to his surprise, Adolfo Bracale agreed: ten thousand a performance, eight performances. Enrico Caruso demanded that the eighty thousand dollars be deposited in his New York bank a month before the tour began. Bracale asked for only one favor: that he sing two matinees at fifty percent of his fee. The tenor replied that he was not in the habit of giving discounts but suggested to the impresario that he include another performance in the contract: officially there would be nine, and he would sing the two matinees for five thousand dollars each.

Waiting for him on the dock in Havana was a group of Italians residing in Cuba, a representative of the president of the republic, a band playing "Vesti la giubba," the impresario Bracale, and the soprano Gabriella Besanzoni, who did not require much pleading to be present to welcome him, given the large number of photographers and reporters who had gathered very early at the berth of the steamship Miami.

Caruso came down the gangplank first, followed by his secretary, Bruno Zirato; his valet, Mario Fantini; another valet, who at one time had been a singer, a pale man called Punzo; and his répétiteur and musical director, Salvatore Fucito. He posed for the cameras with Bracale and with the representative of the president, answered the reporters' questions, was very happy to accept a Havana cigar, which he later gave to the painter Pieretto Bianco, and more than anything else, he perspired. For the two months of his stay in Cuba, Caruso did not stop sweating for an instant, not even when he slept. His perspiring in Havana became an obsession, one more obsession joining the two great obsessions that tormented him at the time.

First, he was concerned about the response of the Cuban audience, rich landowners who had already allowed themselves the luxury of hearing him in his better days, in Milan or New York, and who were ready to pay extremely high prices for their seats, but also ready to be extremely demanding. And second, he was concerned about his safety. Years earlier, the Sicilian Black Hand had threatened to kill him unless he handed over fifteen thousand dollars to the organization. The New York police arrested two Italians, who were tried and sent to Sing Sing prison and subsequently deported. At the time of his visit to Cuba, Caruso still lived with the fear of reprisals, a fear that flared up again when he was handed an anonymous letter on the ship carrying him to Havana. It was a puerile note, which is why he took it seriously. Briefly, it accused him of deceiving the Cuban public and demanded that he cancel the performances at the Teatro Nacional, or else something bad would happen to him. The note was signed "Friends of Hipólito Lázaro," and he had a premonition that the Black Hand had been waiting for just such an opportunity. He gave the letter to the ship's captain and mentioned it to Bracale as soon as they were in the Ford that would drive them to the hotel. Bracale assured him that they had taken precautions at the Sevilla, and several guards would be protecting the security of his six-room suite. Furthermore, President Menocal had ordered the city police to guard the Teatro Nacional. He also offered a bodyguard to accompany the singer as he traveled around Havana, but Caruso said that aside from his professional commitments, he had no intention of going out more than was strictly necessary: his call on the president, two dinners in his honor that had already been announced, and an auction and ball to benefit wounded veterans, which, as it turned out, he did not attend.

As soon as they were in their rooms, and while Caruso was taking a bath, Mario, his valet, told a chambermaid to replace the cotton sheets on the tenor's bed with linen sheets that he refused to give to the woman until she washed her hands. Mario supervised as she changed the sheets, while Punzo was busy handing towels to Caruso, who normally never used hotel towels.

Bruno Zirato, his secretary, was waiting in the sitting room with a handful of telegrams that had preceded the singer to the hotel. Several were from New Orleans and Atlantic City, where the tenor had future performances scheduled; another two telegrams, which he put to one side, were personal: one from Caruso's son Mimmí, who was currently studying at the Culver Military Academy in Indiana; the other from Dorothy, his wife. Zirato read them aloud while Punzo helped Caruso to dress, but in the middle of his reading the secretary could not help exchanging a worried glance with the valet: the tenor coughed and complained twice when he raised his arms. Before reading him the telegram from Dorothy, Zirato suggested he rest for a while, but Caruso refused: Bracale was waiting to take him to the Teatro Nacional. Before rehearsals began, he liked to look over personally the venues he did not know.

Mario handed him his cologne, Acqua di Parma, and Caruso poured it on his hands and patted his perspiring cheeks. He asked the valet if he had brought enough sheets, since it seemed likely that in this heat they would have to be changed several times a day. Mario said he hadn't but would go out immediately and buy more. Caruso made a gesture of annoyance and left the room followed by Zirato, who noticed something else: his employer was lowering one shoulder as he walked, as if trying to compensate for some discomfort, some pain in his side. Fucito and Bracale were waiting for them in the lobby, and the four men climbed into the Ford which drove them to the theater. Zirato carried extra handkerchiefs in his briefcase, but soon after they left, Caruso had soaked them all through. Bracale offered his, saying it was clean. Caruso refused the offer.

They returned to the hotel for lunch after two. The painter Pieretto Bianco was already at the table, as well as most of the Italians who had come to welcome him that morning. Caruso asked for paper and spent the time drawing caricatures, all of which he gave away as soon as they were finished, except for his sketch of a young blond woman who was eating at a nearby table. She asked for his autograph, and Caruso asked her name. On the napkin he drew a cup and wrote in Spanish: "For the beautiful Lydia Cabrera." When the girl went back to her table, Caruso drew her caricature, which was surely the best of them all, and Dr. Castelli, one of the Italians, suggested he donate it to the auction and ball to benefit wounded veterans.

The singer seemed to be in good humor and ate—sirloin steak and pasta—with a hearty appetite; he consumed three glasses of the Italian spumante that Pieretto Bianco had opened, and drank to the success of the performances. Bracale took the opportunity to remark that it might be necessary to postpone the opening scheduled for the tenth of May until the twelfth, because the trunk that contained the scores for the opera Marta had been mislaid on the railways of Florida. Count Tamburini, who was sitting next to the great singer, attempted to make a joke and exclaimed that Marta must be floating somewhere in the Everglades. Bracale smiled, but Caruso stated, in bad temper, that he would tolerate no delays.

He retired to his room at four, and at exactly seven he was ready to leave for his appointment with President Menocal. As he left the hotel and was climbing into the car, a woman stopped him on the sidewalk: a black woman with ashen cheeks and a sunken forehead.

For some reason her eyelids were curled back, or that was the impression Caruso had when he looked at her eyes: he saw the underside of her lids. She tried to touch him, but Bracale stepped between them, and it was over Bracale's shoulder that the black woman shouted the name he had been called back in Naples:

"Errico!"

One of the guards on duty in the hotel came out to the street and moved the black woman away. She spat and cursed before shouting his name for a second time:

"Errico . . . wear white."

Che veggo! Egli?

One of the men working in the kitchen, the one who had been peeling squash, helped us find a taxi. I gave the driver the address, Amargura 75, and then glanced at the theater, cordoned off by police and surrounded by people trying to go in or find out about the injured. Enrico sat beside me, taking deep breaths, sweating into his king's costume, and when the taxi turned onto Paseo del Prado, he asked where we were going.

"To my house," I said, afraid he would change his mind.

"To your house," he murmured, as if he found that hard to believe.

He had a silken voice that seemed to travel up from his stomach, and at the time I supposed he was an actor. I had never been to the theater, only to the movies; I didn't even read the papers, and I couldn't imagine who that man was or where he had come from. I told him my house was close by, and then he asked my name.

"Aida," I answered. "Aida Petrirena Cheng."

"Aïda," he repeated, putting the stress on the *i*, and then he said something I was too ignorant to understand: "Well, just as you see me, I am Radamès."

When we reached my house I paid the driver with the money the cook gave me for the sewing I'd taken to her. Two men passing on the street stopped to look at us; one of them started to laugh at Enrico's costume, and the other stood looking at me as I knocked at the door with gentle little taps so the neighbors wouldn't hear. My mother opened, and her first reaction was to jump back as if she had seen a very handsome devil. Her second reaction was to step forward and pull at me to get me away from that man.

"He's an actor," I told her. "A bomb went off in the theater, and he's in costume."

Enrico held out his hand to her and said his name was Enrico but he wasn't an actor, he was a singer. He was sweating so much that I went to get him a glass of water and a towel. When I came back to the living room, my mother was taking out some shirts and trousers that had belonged to Baldomero. That was when I realized that my dead husband had a similar build: the same barrel chest, the same rib cage that would swell up when he laughed or took a deep breath.

"There are some shoes around here someplace," my mother recalled. "Don't you think he's going to need shoes?"

I said he would, and we left him alone so he could change. We both went to look in the closet where we still kept some of Baldomero's things and all the clothes that had belonged to my little girl who died.

"There was an explosion," I told her in a quiet voice so Enrico couldn't hear me. "It was just like my godfather said. Now we're going to Regla."

My mother sat down on the bed. She complained that she was very tired, and I asked her to lie down for a while.

"I can't," she stammered. "I want to stay with you, I want to know how this all turns out."

She was talking in a strange way, as though she had stones on her tongue. We returned to the living room, Enrico's back was to us, he was disguised as Baldomero, dressed in his shirt and trousers. It seemed to both of us that we were in the past again, and my mother looked at me and crossed herself in terror.

"We have to go to my godfather's house," I told Enrico. "It's the safest place."

He took off his sandals and began to put on the shoes that had belonged to my husband, but first he looked inside; maybe he was surprised they were new. The truth is that Baldomero never even got to wear the shoes: we put them on him when he was dead, for the funeral, and took them off before he was buried. My mother put them away in a box, and we never thought about them again until that Sunday.

"I have to write something," Enrico said. "Do you have paper and ink?"

He spoke slowly so we could understand him. Some words weren't very clear, but my mother, who was very clever about understanding hard languages—she hadn't been married to a Chinaman for nothing—found a piece of paper and the pencil she used to mark down measurements for our customers. She also brought him a clean towel, and he wrapped it around his neck.

"It's for my throat," he said. "I don't want to catch a chill."

Baldomero's shoes were too big for him, but still they were better than the sandals he'd been wearing when he ran out of the theater. He wrote a note and asked my mother to take it to the Hotel Sevilla, place it personally in the hands of Señor Bruno Zirato, and wait for an answer. He said he ought to hide for a few days until they found out who had tried to kill him.

"Take him to Regla," my mother pleaded, tugging at my arm. "Hurry, go to your godfather's house."

She seemed happy about giving him Baldomero's things, including a Panama hat that had been his favorite. Enrico put it on right away, as if he had owned it his whole life, or as if he had lost it a while ago and finally found it in the place he least expected. The two of us left for the Muelle de Luz, the pier where the motorboats docked, the launches that made the crossing to the village of Regla. While I was walking beside him, it occurred to me that he didn't look like an actor or a singer anymore, he didn't even look like a foreigner. He was just somebody from Calle Amargura, a white man walking with a colored woman, a light-skinned mulatta who had a lot of Chinese in her. Enrico had to shuffle in those shoes, and he got tired very fast and suggested we find another taxi, but at that time of day and in that neighborhood there weren't any: just some charcoal sellers pushing their wheelbarrows, and people coming home late from work. There were also some children playing in the empty lots, one of them came over to ask us for money, and that was when Enrico took my arm. We walked a long way, and when we finally could see the ocean he asked what I had been doing in the Hotel Inglaterra when the bomb exploded.

I explained that I worked as a seamstress and that before I got to the Inglaterra to give her clothes to the cook I'd already made some deliveries on Calle Compostela. I didn't dare tell him that everything that had happened was written, that five months before, on the morning of the Feast of the Wise Men, my godfather had read in the *ékuele* that a man would come to crown me. And I didn't tell him that early in May, just at the time of the first thunder, the *babalawo* Yuan Pei Fu had seen him arriving in the middle of dragons and sticks of incense, had seen him stop and take on the form of his body in the powerful smoke of Sanfancón.

"We have to go to the other side," I said, pointing at the bay.

He didn't seem very happy about boarding the motorboat, but he got in, and he went to sit in the most isolated spot. Not many people were traveling with us at that time of day, mostly fishwives and a lot of blacks going home after spending the day in Havana. Enrico stared at the water, and during the crossing it seemed to me he was failing, he was breathing like a sick man, and he didn't look at anybody until the boat stopped and we stepped onto the dock.

Calazán lived pretty far away, almost on the outskirts of town. Around his house, back in those days, there was nothing but woods, and I found my way by keeping my eye on a certain ceiba tree. But it was growing dark, and I had a hard time seeing the ceiba. I told Enrico I had to find a certain tree in order to find the house, and that was when I saw the light, a little light moving toward us along the path. Behind that light, the light of a kerosene lamp, I could see the figure of Calazán, who stopped right in front of us, his bad-tempered face sweating beneath his hat.

"Rain's coming," he grumbled, pointing at the heavy black clouds. "Let's get to the house."

Enrico turned pale, and when we tried to follow Calazán, he stumbled and fell to his knees. He stumbled, or his legs folded under him. He looked so weak my godfather offered his arm for him to lean on. And that's how he managed to stagger to the house, and as soon as we reached it Calazán took him to a room, showed him a narrow iron bed, and told him to lie down. In a matter of seconds Enrico had become sick, and he was pressing his hand to his belly, groaning to himself, without any sound, loud or soft, coming from his mouth. A woman who was in the house, another of my godfather's goddaughters, offered to help me undress him. Between the two of us we took off his sopping-wet shirt and his shoes. Calazán went to the kitchen, and the woman left to find a blanket. I was afraid to stay alone with Enrico, I had never seen anybody so desperate, with his eyes rolled back and that open mouth where no words could come out, only emptiness, only a gust of pain without shape or direction. My godfather came back with a bowl of tea he had brewed, and the two of us lifted Enrico's head so he could drink. It still took a long time before he found relief, and when he finally could talk he said he had felt a horrible stabbing pain, a pain like a nail that wouldn't let him breathe. Calazán nodded and said that now he should sleep; at dawn, if he wanted, he could go back to Havana and see a doctor; but he could also stay there and take country medicines and try to placate the *orishas*, they were the saints who came to our defense because there was no health without a head, no smile without the forgiveness of the dead.

I took my godfather aside and told him that this man was alive by the grace of God; that he had escaped the explosion but still had to be suffering the shock of the noise and smoke.

"I don't know why you're surprised," Calazán said. "I told you months ago and now I'll tell you again: a part of him is already dead, and that part is calling to the other part. All of him is going to die, and it must not happen here."

The woman who had helped me undress Enrico came to say goodbye to my godfather. She was a skinny, mournful creature, who asked for his blessing and kissed his hand. He clutched at her arm:

"Tomorrow you'll go to Santiago de las Vegas, find Señor Calvino, and buy dog herb. Buy as much as you can."

His goddaughter nodded and took the bills Calazán gave her. When she left, he told me this herb would help him relieve the sick man for a time. Not forever, but for a few months until he got to where he had to go, where he had to be in order to die. I asked where he had to die, and he said it was supposed to be in Cuba, but thanks to his intercession with the *orishas* they had arranged for him to die somewhere else, in a place by the sea that once had fire. That was all he could understand of the mysterious words that had come to him from the *ékuele*. Then I wanted to know why dog herb was called by that name and he explained that when it was fresh, it looked like it was raising its ears, those were the seed tassels it had next to the leaves, and it lowered them when it was cooked. It wasn't from Cuba but had been brought here from far away. Señor Calvino was a foreigner who grew herbs of the world and herbs of this country; he showed the herbs of the world to Calazán, he explained if they had poison or power. And Calazán taught him about the herbs of this country, he told him how they had to be planted and which saint had to give permission before they could be picked. This is how they became friends, and sometimes this man Calvino visited him in Regla, or my godfather traveled by horse to Santiago de las Vegas and spent the day with him, teaching him about the things of the countryside.

That night I slept on a cot at the foot of Enrico's bed. I heard him snoring and tossing from side to side. His night was restless, but at dawn I could see that he was calmer and sleeping like a baby. My mother came to Regla very early that morning to tell us that Bruno Zirato had been to our house. He had come alone, in an old hired car, dressed like a Cuban so nobody would follow him. He asked her to tell his employer to stay where he was until they let him know there was no more danger. He also gave her some newspapers for him, and a package of clothes and cigarettes, and an envelope with money.

My mother left without seeing Enrico; he was still asleep. Before she left she wanted to talk to Calazán. I saw them go out of the house, and my mother talked but Calazán refused to say a word. When she got tired of talking and asking and not getting any answers, she turned and walked away. She was crying.

I made breakfast for my godfather and me. We gave Enrico the same tea he drank the night before, and we heated an herbal bath for him. When he put on his own clothes, I picked up

Baldomero's things to wash them, but my godfather told me to leave them be, he said he had to bury them.

Enrico counted the money and insisted on giving part of it to Calazán for putting him up in his house. He also tried to give me some bills, but I refused to accept them and he said he'd give me a present later on. He seemed to feel much better and asked if I could read him the papers. In those days I didn't read very well, I was afraid of making a mistake, so I began in a quiet voice. The newspapers talked about the bomb, they said someone had tried to kill Enrico Caruso and the police were looking for those responsible. Each time he heard his name he closed his eyes and turned pale. Then, with his eyes closed, he asked me to read in a louder voice.

After a while Calazán interrupted us. He said he had something important to say, something I ought to hear too. My godfather had a very complicated way of talking to people, he would go round and round in circles before letting you know what he wanted. He sat down on a footstool and leaned toward Enrico.

"We have to do *ebbó* this week," he began. "Doing *ebbó* is placating the saints. We'll do it so you can get up from this bed, so you can cross the ocean and go back to where you belong, so they'll open a path for you without blood, without sickness." Enrico didn't answer, and Calazán put a hand on his shoulder: "Before doing *ebbó*, I have to ask the saints what they want to eat. I'll go to the *babalochas*, and they'll ask the question for me."

There was a silence, with both of them very serious, and my godfather, with that seriousness on his face, stood up, pulled down his white cap tight on his head, and walked to the door.

"If your mother comes," he said to me from the doorway, "tell her not to do anything. Tell her to wait for me."

He hurried out and I had a premonition, like a stone hitting me in the mouth. I got up and went after him.

"What's my mother coming for? Tell me, Godfather."

Calazán frowned and looked at me, offended. Nobody ever talked to him in that tone.

"Your mother will come to take you back with her to Havana."

I lowered my eyes and waited for the rest.

"She doesn't like it that you're here," Calazán added. "But you're not a little girl, you're a widow, and you know about life. Orula has said you have to stay here till I'm finished. If you don't stay I won't be able to help him, much less you."

I walked slowly back to the room, and Enrico asked me to explain what my godfather wanted. I began by telling him that my godfather didn't want anything, that the saints were the ones who were asking for their offerings and that was why they had to do *ebbó*, which meant giving them food and drink, greeting them and letting them have a good time. Sometimes, besides doing *ebbó*, there were drums. My godfather's godchildren would come and there was a great feast: six drummers began to play at midday and stopped when the sun went down. They couldn't begin any earlier or stop any later. The drum called Añá was the messenger. Enrico asked whose messenger, and I said the messenger of children who wanted to talk to their parents. I told him that even though he was white, he also had to be the son of some *orisha*.

I must have sounded sad because he asked if anything was wrong, and I said my mother wanted me to go back to Havana. He took me by the hand and asked what it was that I wanted to do. I told him I wanted to stay with him until he felt well again and was out of danger; I had promised to take him to a safe place, and I couldn't leave him alone now. Then he asked if I was single, and I had to tell him about Baldomero, about the few years we had to be happy together, about my little girl who died. I couldn't tell him everything because I began to cry, and Enrico sat down on the bed and put his arms around me. "Aïda," he whispered, and he stroked my hair. I put my arms around him too, I put my arms around him and I could smell his cologne; it came from a green bottle packed in the bundle with his clothes.

"Aïda," Enrico said again.

Then I raised my face and he kissed my eyes. I felt as if my eyes melted away into two hot tears that slid down my throat and went from there to my lips, where they turned back into what they had been.

I opened my eyes, I don't know, maybe I opened my mouth. And it was like a veil pulled away from my eyes, like I was seeing everything for the first time.

In 1952 my mother was almost sixty years old, her memory was clear, and, more than anything else, she seemed determined to tell me the truth. And yet the first thing I did to corroborate her story was to check the newspapers from that time.

In those days I was working at a radio station. As a very young girl I had been a reader in a cigar factory. I was the first woman reader in all of Cuba, thanks to the persistence of a neighbor who had once heard me read and said my voice and diction were very good for that kind of work. This neighbor sold leaf tobacco; he would often visit the cigar factories, and he knew the cigar makers, the bosses who hired the readers. That's how he got me the job, which wasn't easy because I was a woman, though I was lucky because the man who let me try out had quite a few daughters and liked me because I resembled one of them. In a cigar factory you could read novels as well as newspapers, and sometimes they asked for poetry. The important thing was to entertain the crowd of workers whose jobs were so monotonous. But sooner or later the natural destiny of every reader was radio, and my dream was to stand in front of a microphone and stay there for the rest of my life. At the age of twenty-four, I achieved my dream. I insisted and pleaded so much that they let me read for them, and one fine day I got a call and was hired by RHC-Blue Network.

I started out reading commercials: for soap, for cold remedies, even for soda crackers. In time they began to use me on soap operas, in supporting roles, almost always playing older women. I was young, but I had a husky voice that sounded very mature. And that became my specialty: mothers-in-law, grandmothers, housekeepers. That March, when my mother got sick and began to tell me her story, I was playing my first important role, practically the lead: the part of Ketty Villada, a widow who falls in love with an employee in her own factory.

At noon, when I finished playing Ketty, I would go straight to the library to read the newspaper reports on the bomb. Using those papers, I first wrote a summary; I constructed a kind of puzzle based on the notes I was taking from different sources. I made a chart of Caruso's arrival, the people who received him in Havana, his first days in the capital, the little anecdotes that were told about him; I even copied down the jokes made at his expense, the vicious remarks, the biting criticism. These notes, in turn, gave me another idea: I would locate people who had been in the theater that afternoon; the reporters who had written about the explosion; the employees of the Hotel Sevilla. One of the first people I decided to interview was a society reporter named Arturo Cidre. The long piece he had written for La Discusión indicated that he had seen the men who placed the bomb, and so I thought he might also have other information that hadn't been written down and could fit somehow into the story my mother was telling me.

Finding Cidre proved to be easier than I had anticipated. As easy as opening the phone book and looking up his name. I called him and we made an appointment. Three days later I went to his apartment on Calle Infanta; he greeted me in that presumptuous tone of voice I had noticed on the phone, and led me directly to the balcony.

I don't know how old he was at the time, but he looked very old to me; I didn't expect him to be so old. Still, he assured me he remembered every detail of what had happened that day. I asked him to speak slowly because I was going to write everything down. Cidre's hands—they were heavily freckled—trembled, and his voice was trembling too. He began to speak and I began to write, I missed a few words but when he was finished I read my notes to him, and he filled in what I needed. He asked where I planned to publish this, and it made me sad to tell him I wasn't planning to publish it at all; I made up a story about working for a man who was going to write a book. This is what Cidre told me:

It was the thirteenth of June, 1920. Write that down carefully, because over the years other dates have been mentioned, but the only date is the one I'm telling you: the bomb went off on Sunday the thirteenth.

I went to the theater alone that afternoon. I had been asked to do an article on the performance, which was his last one in Havana: a matinee at popular prices, sponsored by the Tourism Commission. The auditorium of the Nacional was crowded with people, and Señorita Georgina Menocal, the president's younger daughter, who was sitting in the presidential box, certainly recognized me and waved from a distance. I remember that I settled into my seat, took out a notebook, and sat waiting for the curtain to go up. That was when I looked at the ceiling, at the enormous chandelier they had hung in the center of the hall just a few months earlier. It had caused quite a stir because people thought it might fall on the public at any time. But the scandal died down, and now nobody paid any attention to it. Still, I looked, and in the space where the beams crossed that held up the chandelier, I saw three men moving around.

I was afraid they were up to no good. In my mind I could see the chandelier falling, I saw blood and smoke, I could hear screaming. I left my seat and ran along the aisles and into the lobby, and identified myself to one of the ushers. I told him I was Arturo Cidre, the famous journalist, and that I needed to talk to one of the directors of the Galician Center, the organization that owned the theater. In a few minutes he appeared, a bald man who seemed very nervous. I told him what I had seen, and he ordered several subordinates to go and investigate, but when they went up, the space where the beams cross was deserted. Since the performance was about to begin, I returned to my seat. From time to time I looked up at the chandelier; I couldn't stop looking there.

The first act of Aïda took place without incident. But in the second act, almost at the moment of Radamès' triumphal entrance, when the famous mezzo Gabriella Besanzoni, who was singing Amneris, and María Luisa Escobar, in the role of Aïda, were both onstage, there was a huge explosion. I looked in horror at the chandelier and jumped to my feet, thinking it was about to fall, but it held firm. What fell instead were stones, chunks of plaster, pieces of wood. Escobar and Besanzoni disappeared from view in a downpour of rubble that fell from the arch over the stage. For a moment you couldn't hear anything but the echo of the explosion, and then the shouting began. We were all shouting, I was shouting, too, shouting for order and shouting for help. A woman fell at my feet, bleeding from her nose and some place on her head, I helped her to stand and found myself covered in blood.

One man knew how to keep everyone calm. I remember his name because I interviewed him later: Antonio Henry, a cornetist in the municipal band. He was waiting to play in the corps of trumpeters who lead Radamès' procession, and in the middle of all that confusion he raised his trumpet and began to play the national anthem. Several musicians from the orchestra joined him. People stopped pushing and shoving; the anthem stopped them cold and made them remember they weren't animals. And then the theater employees could finish opening all the doors and have us leave in an orderly fashion.

When I was out on the street, I started asking about the sopranos. I thought they might be dead. But no, both had escaped. Besanzoni, dressed in her elaborate tunic, left by the back door of the theater and ran down Calle Consulado, where she had the good fortune to meet a young man, Manuel Martínez, who took her to a nearby café and gave her some cognac to calm her nerves. I interviewed this Manuel Martínez later on; I think he fell in love with Besanzoni: can you imagine what it means to a man to run into an Egyptian princess on the street and have that princess, with lips trembling and breasts exposed, collapse into his arms? Caruso ran away too, but nobody could tell me where he had gone. One of the ushers in the theater said he had seen him get into a taxi, still wearing his Radamès costume. But Manuel Martínez himself assured me that while he was fanning Señorita Besanzoni, he saw the great tenor cross the street and go through a little door that he later found out was the door to the kitchen of the Hotel Inglaterra.

I went there to make inquiries. The cook, a terrifying woman, assured me that Enrico Caruso had never come into her kitchen and neither had any other performer. There were two men who were her helpers; they didn't look at me, but I sensed they knew something and weren't talking because they had been warned not to by that formidable matron who was cutting up rabbits.

That same night, all the reporters, myself included, went to the Hotel Sevilla. We met with Bruno Zirato, who was Caruso's secretary, and Adolfo Bracale, the impresario who had brought the singer to Cuba. Zirato said that Caruso had not been injured but couldn't be interviewed yet because he was still suffering from shock.

The correspondent for the Associated Press, a quiet, clever boy who had been a student of mine for a time, asked if it wasn't true that the Sicilian Black Hand had threatened to kill Caruso. Zirato replied that the investigation was in the hands of the Cuban police. Another reporter, from the Diario de la Marina, wanted to know if it was true that Caruso had run into the Parque Central, where he had been pursued by a crowd of hooligans who made fun of his earrings and bracelets, and had to be rescued, in a state of absolute hysteria, by the police. Zirato smiled and said that Caruso hadn't gone anywhere near the park. Then I asked the only question that made him lose his self-assurance: had the great tenor, by any chance, gone into the kitchen of the Hotel Inglaterra?

Zirato quickly denied this, but was so shaken I guessed I had hit a sore spot. He admitted to the reporters that Caruso had not had time to change his clothes and, at the urging of the theater employees, who told him his life was in danger, had run out onto the street still dressed as Radamès. According to him, it was a private citizen, a physician driving by in his car, who offered to take him to the Hotel Sevilla—certainly not the Inglaterra—where he arrived safe and sound, though extremely agitated.

The police inquiry took place in the theater, and I had to make a statement regarding what I had seen: the three figures moving along the beams that held up the chandelier. But the bomb had not been set there; if it had, I would not be here today talking to you. It had been placed in the washrooms of the upper balcony, near the arch over the stage. It had not exploded in the audience because it was not meant to. I know that thirty people were hurt, and some suspects were arrested, including a pharmacist from El Cerro and his two daughters, as well as two sailors from a ship docked in the port, and several other people.

In the course of the investigation it came to light that the theater management and even the police had known about the attempt ahead of time, as demonstrated by the fact that the entrances to the Nacional were guarded that afternoon, and the district police chief was also on the premises. But the people who set the bomb, whoever they were, knew how to get in without raising anyone's suspicions.

Enrico Caruso disappeared for several days. Some said he locked himself in his room at the Sevilla, others that he left for New York. But a certain man whom I finally persuaded to talk to me, and whose name I promised never to reveal, told me that the Commendatore fled to Regla, the home of brujos and santeros, the last place on earth anyone would think of looking for him. From there he traveled to Matanzas, where he walked into the Lagoon of San Joaquín, a lagoon that's used for purging and purification and God knows what other superstitions. Can you imagine the great Caruso stripping naked in a crowd of babalawos, singing with them and allowing them to pass a pigeon between his legs? He finally resurfaced in Santa Clara, at the home of the Berenguers. From there he wrote to Dorothy, his wife, who had also just suffered a severe shock because thieves had broken into their house and stolen all her jewelry. It was rumored that these were not ordinary thieves but the hired thugs of the Black Hand.

Caruso left Cuba at the end of June, and I was the only journalist who interviewed him before his departure. I bribed the crew and officers to let me onto the steamship Cartago shortly before it sailed. In the dining room, which was deserted at that time of day, I found the great tenor, or the little that was left of him. I was very *affected by what I saw: he was sitting at a table, with his head in his hands, murmuring this sentence over and over again: "Chi me l'ha fatto fare? Chi me l'ha fatto fare?" His shirt was soaked through, as if he had just been pulled from the water, and his jacket had fallen to the floor. I thought he must be drunk, but he wasn't. When I spoke to him, he put out his cigarette and tried to smile. The expression on his face reminded me of how he had played Pagliacci: the same agony, the same distorted grimace of despair. For a moment I thought he would be angry to see me there, that he would take it out on me, but I realized he was very far away just then, or at least far removed from petty matters.*

We talked for half an hour. Slowly, he spoke to me of his plans and said he was on his way to Mexico City, then New Orleans and several other cities. One of the few enthusiasms of his life at the time was the thought of singing in the middle of the jungle, in a place called Iquitos, where a certain Señor Fitzgerald was building a great theater and wanted him to give the opening performance. He referred to the first Radamès he had ever played, in a theater in Moscow, and confessed that he had never seen more beautiful hands than those of Salomea Kruheniska, the soprano who sang with him on that occasion. One subject led to another, and he recalled that the diva Tetrazzini was also in Moscow that season; she called him "my plump little darling" and would massage his temples with cologne. . . . Now, when his head was splitting, he would have given anything to have a woman's hands, Kruheniska's hands, for instance, massaging his temples.

I knew Caruso wasn't saying all that just for me. I understood that a part of the man had given up, or perhaps that all of him was on the verge of collapse. Zirato and Fucito came to the dining room and realized it had been a serious mistake to leave Caruso alone: there I was, an important journalist, picking up the pieces, observing his definitive decline. Zirato turned red and asked me to excuse them, since the Commendatore *had to return to his state-room.*

When I left the ship, I felt as if I had been infected by his immense sadness. I was desperate for a drink, some conversation. I went to the Aires Libres, a sidewalk café on the Paseo del Prado, which always took me back to the cafés of Paris, but this time I felt as if I weren't in Paris but at the bottom of a pit. I promised myself I wouldn't write a word of what I had seen.

I kept my promise; I never wrote it down until now, and now I'm not even the one who's writing, the person writing everything is you.

Oh! chi lo salva?

Two days later my mother came back to Regla, walked into the room where I was taking care of Enrico, and said she had to talk to me. When we had gone out, she smoothed my hair and whispered: "Poor Aida, you're already a widow, what other trouble are you looking for?" I covered my face with my hands and discovered I couldn't cry. The sorrow of death can do that, it can dry you up sometimes: when you need them most, no tears come to your eyes, there's only grief clawing at your stomach, a scorpion under the stone of your heart.

I never knew if that was when my mother guessed or if Calazán had told her I'd been kissing Enrico. If she guessed, she didn't have time for any more reproaches because Calazán, who had left a little earlier with one of his godsons, came back very upset and said that some strangers were in Regla. We were standing in the doorway of the house, it was a cloudy afternoon, and right behind Calazán were some of his older godsons: four blacks who looked like stevedores, and their friends—there must have been ten or twelve of them—who had come to protect us. One of Calazán's godsons also had a pistol—the others were carrying machetes—and it was the one with the pistol who walked with my mother down to the little boat that would take her back to Havana. Before she left she stroked my face and said she wasn't afraid to leave me there because with the grace of the *orishas* and my godfather's protection, nothing bad could happen to me.

We didn't tell Enrico just then that the men who were after him were in Regla. My mother had brought another parcel of clothes from his secretary, and some liquids for him to gargle with, and a box filled with cigarettes. He didn't know the house was surrounded by men guarding him, Calazán's godsons who'd kill before they let a foreigner near us. Still, it wasn't a foreigner who fell but a Cuban, a one-eyed mulatto who came to the house at nightfall, claiming he was looking for his sister. Calazán greeted him, let him think he believed him, and asked him in. When he was inside the house the guards attacked him, searched his pockets, roughed him up, and the next thing I knew his mouth was bleeding and he was swearing by his mother that he didn't know what they were talking about. They beat him some more and still he didn't know. In the end he had no choice, he had to talk, his tongue loosened as soon as he felt the noose: one of the godsons tightened it around his neck and whispered that Regla belonged to Calazán, that nothing would happen to them if they tied a stone to his waist, put him in a sack, and threw him into the bay. The man was scared to death and admitted he'd been sent by some Italians who wanted to know if that was the house where the singer Enrico Caruso was hiding, how many people lived there, and what they would have to do to get him out and take him back to Havana. When he heard that, Calazán moved his godsons away and stood in front of the man: he had to tell the foreigners that nobody set foot in Regla without his permission, and starting at twelve o'clock that night, if he found out that one of them was sneaking around town he would track him down with the *ñáñigos* of his brotherhood, cut off his privates and cut out his tongue, and when he was missing two pieces of his body he'd be turned over to the barracks in Regla, where another of his godsons was in charge.

The man stood up, he didn't look back or say he was sorry. For now he knew they'd given him the chance to deliver the message, and none of my godfather's godsons would hurt him. Enrico and I watched him through the window when he left. Enrico wanted to know what was going on and I lied and told him it was a thief. In a little while my godfather came in and said we could rest easy, no place was safer than the village of Regla, where he was the only man in charge. Then he told us the day had been fixed for doing *ebbó* to Yemayá, and it wouldn't be in Regla but at a lagoon in Matanzas. After we had fulfilled our obligations to the saints—that was his favorite word: obligations—we could both leave in peace.

That night, at supper, Enrico talked about the ocean. For the first time in my life I heard of a city called Naples. He told me that when he was a boy he wanted to be a sailor, and a barber, a friend of his father's, promised to teach him to sail. The barber, before he was a barber, had been a helmsman and had sailed around the world. He'd brought back a marble egg from one of his voyages, and whenever he had to shave an old man he would put the egg in his mouth to make his cheeks taut. When he took out the egg he would put it back in his pocket without washing it, then pull it out again for the next old man, and for the next, and the last old man would swallow the saliva of everybody who'd been shaved before him. Enrico learned to do the same thing, but he used chicken eggs. He'd put an egg in his mouth and try to bring his lips together without breaking it; according to the barber, this exercise strengthened the muscles and tuned the voice. A sailor needed a tuned voice just like a singer did. Enrico was a singer.

In those days in Naples, people were dying of combination fevers. Typhus would combine with cholera and dysentery, and the result was called "Neapolitan fever." Two of his brothers, who'd been born before Enrico, died when they were little, and if he didn't die too, or get sick from the sulfur disinfectant they threw in the streets, or lose his voice or his teeth from breathing in the fumes, it was because his mother arranged for a stronger, better-fed woman to nurse him for the first few months of his life. Enrico still remembered his wet nurse. When he lived in Naples he would visit her. He never forgot the shape of her body or the taste of her breast, and I think he was sincere when he said he couldn't believe that in a village like Regla, so far away and so full of blacks, he'd found that taste again, the food that had nourished him when he was a baby. He said this as he touched me under my blouse, and then he got gloomy because he thought the coincidence was a warning: his life would end in the place where it had begun. He asked me to look into his face and tell him what I saw. I said that I saw his face, and he said no. "Everything's over," he said. "You're the end." I was twenty-seven then, though I probably looked thirty. Until that time I had been with only one man: Baldomero Socada. But in all those years I had never seen any man cry. Enrico was crying, in silence; that's when a person cries from the heart, the tears flow without stopping and there's no expression on his face, he doesn't move a muscle. I watched him cry for a long time, and when I saw there were no more tears, I took off my clothes and lay down beside him. He put his hand on my stomach, and I told him to sleep. But he didn't sleep, he said the same thing again, that I was his end, and then, to calm him, I told him the truth: his end wasn't in Cuba; my godfather had read it in the *ékuele*. We stayed awake and watched the dawn, the first light that comes like a quiet stream of cool water. Sometime during the night he said that Regla smelled like Naples, that the bed where he was lying had the same smell as his mother's bed. I asked him if his mother was still alive, and he said she had died when he was fifteen, and it was on the afternoon she died that his voice changed. He was singing in a church choir and felt a heat rise in his throat: that was the heat that gave his voice a different tone. When he finished singing, a woman came up and told him in a whisper that he should hurry back to his house. Enrico understood and burst into tears. The heat came and went, and until he was eighteen he didn't know if he was going to be a tenor or a baritone. He explained to me what it meant to be one thing and what it meant to be the other. He sang a passage like a baritone and then he said he would sing like a tenor, which is what he was.

He began slowly, and his voice didn't seem to come out of his mouth, it was like a hum rising up from the ground, and it became strong and filled everything, like a tremor in the air. The first thing I heard in that song was my name. Ifá doesn't lie, Ifá is never wrong, and my godfather was a simple interpreter of Ifá. The *orishas* had blown that melody through the *ékuele*, and the music stayed in my life forever. Years later, when I had the record and could buy a phonograph to play it on, the first thing I did in the morning, before I had coffee and before I washed my face, was play that song. Enrico's voice would run through my veins again, it was a melody that hurt me and made me despair, and that despair allowed me to live.

At the time he came to Cuba, Enrico was married, and he had a little girl just a few months old, whose name was Gloria. He talked to me about Gloria but not about his wife, I found out later she was an American the same age as me. The woman he did talk about was the mother of his two older children. Ada Giachetti was a singer too, but she never married Enrico because she was already married when she met him. At first I thought she had died because of the way he described her absence, but one night he told me that Ada had left them, him and their children, and when that happened his voice changed again. He didn't feel any heat in his throat, this time it was a stabbing cold, a pain like ice breaking one of his vocal cords.

I never was jealous of his American wife. I never once thought about that woman. But I was tormented by Ada Giachetti, or her memory, which amounts to the same thing. She still torments me, even now when her bones have turned to dust. Dust that was loved by Enrico. He looked for her in other women: he looked for her in Ada's sister, whose name was Rina, and he looked for her in his American wife, whose name, I found out, was Dorothy. And finally he looked for her in me, not all the time, but he did at the beginning. He said I had teeth like Ada's. That was the only way I could be like her, because I was a mulatta who had her father's Chinese eyes and a nose that came from the Lucumi part. I was a combination, as mixed as Neapolitan fever. My life was made of different kinds of heat, and I tried to warm Enrico with that heat. And I did, at least a little, until the day he walked onto the ship that took him away from Havana forever.

That was the day I learned that Calazán had read more in the *ékuele* than he'd told me: he read that I would meet Enrico and fall in love with him. But he also read that I was destined to go with him, follow him to the place of his death, no matter if he died in Cuba or in Naples: I was supposed to end where he ended.

Calazán saw it all so clear that he closed his eyes. But even though his eyes were closed, the sign of Ikú appeared to him, which is like seeing death appear, and that's what he told my mother. If they asked me to bring them the man who had come to crown me, if they took in Enrico Caruso and protected him from the men who were after him, it wasn't to save him but me. When they separated us in Cuba, they separated me from the darkness he was destined to give me, the sorrows we were going to share. They separated my skin from my flesh, my bones from my blood, my heart from its feeling. But they couldn't do anything about what I had inside. That too was written, and Orula ordered them not to touch it. It was Orula who ordered that you live, Enriqueta. That's why I'm telling you this story.

*I*n the middle of April, shortly after I had interviewed Arturo Cidre, I paid a visit to Manuel Martínez, who lived on the roof of a building on Calle Lealtad, in a small structure made of bricks: two rooms divided by a shower curtain. Next to it was a pigeon coop, a shack made of rough boards. When I knocked at the door, I heard wings fluttering behind the boards, and from inside the coop a man's voice answered.

"I was sent by Arturo Cidre," I said. "I'd like to ask you about Enrico Caruso."

The man looked out. "I don't know anything about Caruso."

"I've come to ask you about the day the bomb went off," I insisted.

"I don't know anything about that either."

He came out of the coop, his shirt unbuttoned. He was holding a dead pigeon, which he wrapped in newspaper and tossed into a corner. Manuel Martínez was a phantom, with a fragile-looking skull and eyes devoured by rancor: the mere ghost of a man. He asked me in, and we sat at a table that held two large pails filled with corn. From there I could see the faded photograph that reigned over the disorder. I didn't have a moment's doubt: it was a picture of Gabriella Besanzoni.

"Her," said Manuel, pointing at the photograph. "I only know about her."

Something white and fluffy—it was pigeon down—was sticking

to the damp skin of his arms and neck, and his shirt and trousers bore the marks of the coop: dried or recent shit, feathers distorted by the light, the remains of feed.

"I'm the assistant of a professor who's planning to write a book," I lied; never in my life had I told a lie in so sincere a voice.

"What do you want to know?"

"Everything you can remember," I replied. "I want to know what happened that day."

I showed him my notebook, and he made a gesture of annoyance. I don't know if at some point he thought of asking me to leave his house. His breathing was labored, perhaps from emotion, and he looked so worn out I was about to tell him I'd come back another day. But something stopped me; it was the first thing he said, a sentence I later understood as the key to everything that had happened: "The real bomb was the one that destroyed us inside."

I asked him to speak slowly, and I began to copy down his words.

I hardly remember Caruso, my clear memory is of Gabriella. It was the thirteenth of June, the year was 1920—mark that down date, because other dates have been mentioned. I was walking up Calle San Miguel toward Zulueta, on my way to the house of my fiancée. In those days I was managing a warehouse, a huge warehouse filled with garlic and herrings. I earned good money and was saving to get married.

I didn't hear the explosion, I didn't hear anything. Two men ran past me, they looked very excited, they were shouting, but I didn't pay attention to what they were saying. When I got to the place where Calle Consulado divides, I saw a woman rushing out of the back of the theater, a whirlwind of veils and bracelets, all alone, coming toward me like a vision. I noticed her clothes: she was wearing a costume, a tunic embroidered in gold, and a strange crown on her head. A strap on the tunic had come loose and one of her breasts was exposed, but she didn't seem to notice. I looked at that breast as if it were an eye, and that breast looked back at me, but she didn't. She was in no condition to look at anybody, or listen to anybody; she couldn't even talk. She just came toward me and collapsed.

The sound of her body striking the pavement was the coup de grâce to my whole life. I ran to her and tried to raise her head, I did what I had seen other people do when someone fainted: I patted her lightly on the cheek. She didn't respond and I tried to sit her up, I shook her arms and breathed into her face; there were beads of perspiration above her lips and a kind of fine sand covering her neck. Her arms, too, were dirty with soot and dust, but even so she seemed untouchable, a woman who might vanish at any moment.

She began to regain consciousness; she struggled to her feet, and I asked her name. She told me her name was Gabriella, that there had been an explosion in the theater and something had fallen from the ceiling and hit her on the head, but she couldn't remember how she got out. She said that all she wanted was to go back to her hotel and asked if I could take her there. I removed my jacket and put it around her, we started walking and she took my arm. That's when we saw Caruso, I wouldn't have recognized him, but Gabriella called to him twice, she shouted, "Rico! Rico!" He didn't hear or didn't want to stop. He was dressed as an Egyptian warrior; it was difficult to see what he was wearing from that distance, but that's what the papers said. He looked very frightened and stumbled a few times before he went through a door; I thought it led to a bar, but we found out later, Arturo Cidre and I, that it was the door to the kitchen of the Hotel Inglaterra.

I took Gabriella to a café. At that time of day, fortunately, there weren't many patrons, and the owner brought us a bottle of cognac. When I told him a bomb had exploded in the Teatro Nacional, he asked about Caruso. We told him he was alive because we had just seen him on the street. Gabriella drank her cognac and asked me again to take her to her hotel. And so I walked with her to the Sevilla, and I went up to her room, where she gave me back my jacket, but then she asked me to stay. The thought of the explosion still made her tremble, she said she was very frightened, and I stayed with her all afternoon and all night, all that time and I didn't lay a finger on her, I just watched her sleep and listened to her moan: she was moaning in her sleep. The maid she traveled with took care of keeping other people away, and the impresario Bracale did his best to get rid of the reporters. The only one who knew I was with Gabriella, watching over her in her room, was Arturo Cidre, who may have found out from the maid or one of the waiters. In those days, Cidre was always generous with his tips.

The next day, that was a Monday, I said goodbye to Gabriella and went straight to my job. I went to the warehouse as if nothing had happened, or as if everything were happening for the first time: the routine, the stevedores, all the paperwork when a shipment came in or went out. I was overwhelmed by the smell of garlic and all the different smells of herring, it was as if I had been transformed into a different man, and in the afternoon I went back to the Sevilla, where I found a much calmer Gabriella. She asked me to stay a while, and begged my pardon. The truth was that I didn't know what I had to pardon her for, and I told her so. For having ruined my Sunday afternoon, she said, and for asking me to spend the whole night with her. I answered that if I had run into her a thousand times, I would have stayed with her a thousand times. In the year 1920 I wasn't what I am now, a ragged old man keeping his pigeons. Gabriella came toward me and I let her slide against my body, I let her pour over me as if she were water. I never imagined that her single eye, that nipple that blinked when it saw me, could do me so much harm. She gave me her photograph and said she couldn't *leave Cuba this way. I put my arms around her and proposed that we leave the Sevilla, that we run away, and she agreed.*

I took all my savings and made up a story. I told my parents that the owner of the warehouse was sending me to pick up a shipment of garlic in Matanzas province. And I lied to my fiancée, whose name was Francisca, but she suspected something and asked where I'd be staying, how long I'd be away, who I'd be traveling with. There was little I could tell her. I packed a bag and left with Gabriella. At the age of twenty-two, which was how old I was at the time, you pack a single bag and attempt a single, monumental act of madness. Gabriella was very young too, just a few years older than me, and the bomb had upset her, it had forced her to think about death. Those thoughts were the reason she ran away with me. We didn't get very far. We stopped in the village of Santiago de las Vegas and rented a little house next to the forestry station, a kind of garden tended by an Italian, a botanist named Mario Calvino. He and his wife were thrilled when they learned that the quiet woman they had taken at first for a Russian ballerina was the celebrated Gabriella Besanzoni. We asked them to keep our secret, and the botanist's wife, who was pregnant at the time, told us if they had a girl they would name her Gabriella, and if the baby was a boy they would call him Italo, in honor of their Italy, which was so far away. In any case, they made Gabriella promise that she would baptize the baby. But Gabriella never kept her promise because in a few days we returned to Havana.

I broke off with Francisca and argued with my parents, who by this time knew all about my adventure. There were cables waiting for Gabriella at the Hotel Sevilla, along with letters from her family and offers from impresarios proposing dates and cities. Two nights later she confessed that she wanted to sing in New York, but said she would come back. I knew I was lost and tried to persuade her not to go, and she said she couldn't abandon the opera—opera was her true life. I accompanied her to the ship but secretly I had decided to stop her. When she tried to kiss me goodbye, I raised my hand to her. I slapped her like a savage in front of everyone who was leaving, waving their handkerchiefs on deck, and everyone staying behind. I was in a rage and pushed her as hard as I could, and for the second time I heard the sound of her body falling on paving stones. Some men grabbed my arms, somebody punched me in the face, and Gabriella hurried onto the ship: she didn't want anyone to recognize her.

The next day I went back to my house and talked to my parents. I reconciled with Francisca and married her earlier than planned. And so I went back to my job at the warehouse; it was more crowded than ever with garlic and herring. Gabriella wrote to me often. Once she asked me to meet her in Mexico, she said she would wait for me there, that she hadn't forgotten me. I smelled my arms; garlic on the skin has a strange odor, and it had gotten into my pores: that was my excuse for not wanting to travel. Francisca read the letter and asked me if I was going to leave her. We had a son by then, and she needed to know if I was planning to abandon them. I assured her I wasn't; I said I was too ashamed of my smell.

I often thought that if it hadn't been for the bomb that Sunday, I would have walked past the theater and heard what you could always hear: the echo of the music, and sometimes applause. Nobody would have run out at just the wrong time, no woman in tulle and emeralds, no princess with the eye of her breast blazing. My poor wife Francisca would not have had to suffer the twenty-seven years she suffered with me, having to choke down my nostalgia for Gabriella, letting me hang that photograph and worship it in my hidden grief.

That's why I say the bomb did us more damage on the inside than it ever could have caused in the theater. Caruso ran away in his warrior's sandals, but who cares what happened to Caruso? He went on with his life, but not us. Look at me: Francisca's dead, but *she'd already died long before, another victim killed by the explosion. She wasn't counted among the casualties, and neither was I, but look at my scars, look at that photograph of Gabriella, take a good look: because of her my blood was sucked dry.*

And now excuse me. I have a dead pigeon to throw away.

Si levano gli estinti . . .

*B*lue figs from Sorrento. He said that's what my mouth tasted like. I never knew how those figs tasted because after he died I lost all hope of eating them. Hope and courage: I never left this city again.

Enrico promised to take me to Naples; he promised to take me to Sorrento to eat figs, and when we got tired of eating them we'd go to Milan. In Milan he'd show me a great theater where all they sang was opera, and we'd walk along La Galleria, a street he kept telling me about like it was some kind of dream. He left the best for last: Villa Bellosguardo, his real home. That's where he had his collection of crèches, a whole roomful of mangers. Nobody could touch them but him, nobody dared to interrupt when he was looking at the little figures, thousands of pieces it had taken him years to collect and arrange. He promised that someday he'd let me help him: just once, he said, to sew clothes for the shepherds. We made that agreement and he gave me a drawing of the villa. I wrote the date on it, and I've always kept it. That same afternoon I met Bruno Zirato.

Calazán, who knew about his visit, waited for Zirato on the road along with a group of his godsons, who never left us during this time. When they came into the house Enrico ran to his secretary; he hadn't seen him since the day of the explosion, and they hugged and started talking in Italian. Calazán moved away with his godsons, I think it made him miserable, I'm sure deep down it made him very angry that he couldn't understand what they were saying. I went to the kitchen to prepare coffee. When

I walked into the living room, I found out that Zirato had brought a suitcase; it was half open and I saw it was full of clothes. Another valise was crammed with packs of cigarettes, they weren't Cuban, that was all I knew at first, but later I learned they were Egyptian. It occurred to me that Zirato had come to Regla to take Enrico back with him, and my legs started to tremble and tears came to my eyes. Just at that moment my godfather came in and used a tone of voice I knew very well, the proud, mocking tone he used when he spoke in the name of the warrior *orishas*.

"Why don't you save those tears for when your mother dies?"

For the first time I didn't answer him like his goddaughter, like the obedient girl he had watched growing up; I answered like the widowed and hungry woman I carried inside me.

"I've cried for a lot of dead, Godfather: my grandmother, my father, my husband Baldomero, and my little girl who died. Especially my daughter. Now I'm going to cry for the living. I don't want to be separated from Enrico. He's going to take me to Naples."

Calazán made a face to let me know how angry he was: with the tip of his tongue he pushed out one cheek from the inside, then he refused the coffee I offered him.

"You're a mule. But I put up with it because it was written. Ifá doesn't lie, Ifá is hardly ever wrong."

"I'm a grown woman, Godfather. You said yourself he was coming to crown me. Well, let him: I don't want to die without him crowning me."

"I also told you he was dead, marked by the saint of his head. Nobody can save him, Aida. But maybe I can save you. I owe that favor to your mother, and especially to old Petrona, your Lucumi grandmother. And I owe it to your real father. Now that you're all grown up and think you know so much, I'll tell you the truth: Noro Cheng, your mother's husband, was nothing to you. Your real father is Yuan Pei Fu. *Babalawo* to *babalawo*, I have an obligation to him."

He didn't take his eyes off me, and I didn't look away. By now it didn't surprise me at all that Yuan Pei Fu was my real father. Maybe, deep down, I expected it, and even if I didn't, the only thing I cared about was being with Enrico, staying with him for as long as God let me. A seamstress from Calle Amargura, a simple woman, can't explain certain things. I couldn't explain it then, but every time I went to bed with Enrico, when we had our arms around each other, I didn't feel like he was entering me, the natural way, but just the opposite: I had the feeling his body was coming out of me, that I was giving birth to him as I held him, that he had belonged to me before I knew him. This was a love full of mysteries because Orula had laid on her hand, and the roads were already marked, and our words and suffering were also written.

"Get your things together," Calazán ordered. "We're going to Matanzas."

It still wasn't clear if Enrico would come with us. I didn't feel easy until I took him his coffee and he told me, in front of Zirato, that the men who were threatening him, the ones who had set the bomb in the theater, knew he was in Regla. They were dangerous people, ready to pay a lot of money if they could do him harm. Calazán had suggested another hiding place, just for a few days, until everything got back to normal and he could show his face in Santa Clara.

"Then we'll go to Naples," he told me in a quiet voice. "You'll be with me there."

The next day we left Regla in a fishing boat that belonged to one of Calazán's godsons. Other godsons came sailing behind our boat, making sure nobody could get near us.

When we reached the Muelle de Luz, two cars were waiting. Zirato got into one, and the other—I remember it was a blue Packard (the first time I ever rode in anything so elegant)— was for us: Calazán and the driver up front, Enrico and me in the back, holding hands, touching every once in a while, giving each other kisses that seemed like a serpent's kisses to me, but Enrico said they were desert kisses because they were silent and hot, as though we were kissing through sand, as though we were buried in sand and had become nothing but sand.

It took us almost five hours to get to the house. I could see right away it wasn't a plain house like Calazán's. I never found out who the place belonged to or why it had been chosen for Enrico to hide in. After the Packard went through the big gates at the entrance—they were opened by a very old black man who looked exactly like my godfather—it drove along a road lined with royal palms. Before we even got out of the car, two women came to welcome us. One was Dominga, the same goddaughter who'd been in Regla the night I arrived with Enrico. The other was an old black woman who introduced herself as Conga Mariate, though it turned out she wasn't a Congo woman but a Lucumí and an *iyalocha*, a priestess consecrated in Oyó, which was the land of Olokun.

They had prepared the best room in the house for Enrico, with a double bed and fine mosquito netting. The way the mosquito netting was sewn, and the tulle and ribbons that had been used on it, made me think the bedroom belonged to a woman who was alone, maybe an old woman. Enrico didn't know the name of the place or who the owners were. Only Conga Mariate, who came to look out one of the windows with us, took the trouble to tell us anything at all:

"Over there is Unión de Reyes, and on the other side,

Sabanilla del Comendador. The Lagoon of San Joaquín is beyond those woods you see right there."

She crossed herself and warned that neither of us, not the "French musyú" or the paisana daughter of Sanfancón, ought to go near that water alone. I tried to explain that Enrico wasn't French, and that even though I was Chinese I wasn't the daughter of the Changó of the paisanos but the child of Yemayá, who was my mother and my hope. Conga Mariate paid no attention and kept nodding her head:

"Modu Modu! French musyú!"

Then she walked over to Enrico, who was taking clothes out of his suitcase.

"Musyú, listen: Ogún eats spilled blood."

He turned and looked at her from head to toe. Conga Mariate wore a white turban, and her long dress, her shoes and stockings, were the same color. Her arms were covered with bracelets, most of them white and heavy, the others were thin silver. Around her neck she wore the beads of her founding *orisha:* I'm certain it was Obatalá.

"Get it away, musyú," she said to Enrico, pointing at the pistol he had just found packed in with his underwear. "Hide it; Calazán is doing *Ossode.*"

The black woman left and Enrico closed the suitcase, but he opened it again, took out the gun, looked around, and decided to hide it under the mattress. Then he asked what it was she had said my godfather was doing.

"Doing *Ossode* is when the *babalawo* throws the *ékuele* to find out his future," I told him. "Calazán wants to know what is waiting for him."

We ate early: boiled vegetables and a chicken stew that Dominga cooked. We all sat at the table except Conga Mariate, who was used to eating her food just before the sun went down.

Calazán seemed to be in a good mood; I thought maybe Ifá had told him things that were good for him and, somehow, good for us too. He asked Enrico about his work, and Enrico explained that he sang in the theater, that's what opera was: singing stories instead of sitting down to tell them. Then Calazán asked him to tell us the story he was singing on the afternoon the bomb went off. Enrico smiled and looked at me; I had also asked him to tell me that story.

"The story has Aïda's name," he began, just as the Congo woman came in with the coffee. "It's a story about Africa, where one people made war on another."

"The *vodú* of Dajomi," shouted Calazán, and exchanged a knowing look with the old woman.

"Not them," said Enrico. "It was the Ethiopians and the Egyptians. The Ethiopian slave, called Aïda, loved the warrior Radamès. Amneris, the daughter of the pharaoh, loved Radamès too."

"This Radamès is like Changó," Conga Mariate said with a sigh, and Calazán nodded in silence.

"Amneris owned the slave Aïda, Aïda owned the heart of Radamès, and Radamès owned the hearts of both women. But Aïda's father, who had been taken prisoner in his own land and brought to Egypt, found his daughter and asked her to betray Radamès."

"Allágguna," Calazán said, "that father must be Allágguna, always looking to make trouble."

"His name was Amonasro, and to persuade his daughter he told her their country had been destroyed, their city covered by a sea of blood, and from the black whirlpools in that sea the dead were rising."

"May God forgive them," said Dominga, crossing herself.

"Amneris discovered that Aïda was in love with Radamès.

Mad with jealousy, she called for her slave and threatened her."

"Oshún and Yemayá," was Conga Mariate's comment. "If they're allowed to they kill each other over the same man."

Enrico stopped for a moment and gave her a curious look. Then he stood up to light a cigarette. It was dark by now, and we had lit oil lamps that he said were very bad for his throat. He wanted fresh air, and went over to the window.

"Aïda convinced Radamès that they should run away together. But he was caught and accused of treason. The priests condemned him to be buried alive in a tomb."

"Damn it, that's the *vodú*!" Calazán shouted again. "Don't you see how they punish by going down to the carrion?"

This moved Conga Mariate, and she came over to me and took my hand. Her skin, brushing against mine, was like a rough, dead shell. I was afraid of that shell, afraid of death for the first time. The Congo woman noticed this and began to talk to me in a very low voice:

"Changó didn't know his real mother was Yemayá. He didn't know she was his mother, he wanted her to be his wife. '*Omó mi*,' said Changó, and Yemayá offered him her breast, then Changó recognized her and began to cry."

"Amneris was sorry she had betrayed Radamès," Enrico went on. "She pleaded with the priests to save him, she pleaded with the gods, but none of them had pity. Then she cried over the stone that buried the warrior."

"Oshún didn't know that Changó was her nephew," the Congo woman whispered in my ear. "She didn't know and wanted to be his wife, that's why she came to such a bad end. She cried over a stone too."

"Aïda went into the tomb before Radamès and waited so she could die with him. . . . Together they saw heaven open, they saw the angel of death appear."

"Olofi is great," boomed Calazán's voice, and from the woods we heard the cry of the owl.

Nobody spoke, and nobody moved. As if we were joined together, our souls or whatever it was that could be joined with that love magic from Africa. I remembered that my godfather, Josè de Calazán, hadn't heard the song yet, the song that said my name; he hadn't heard it with his ears, he had only received it into his hands the day he threw the *ékuele* for me. That's why I asked Enrico to sing it, for me and for Calazán, for Conga Mariate and for Dominga. To sing it loud so they could hear it in the woods and beyond the mountain, in Unión de Reyes and in Sabanilla del Comendador.

Enrico walked around the table and stopped again by the window. From there he asked me to turn off the lamps, and Conga Mariate and I turned off all of them. We were in the dark except for the light from the countryside, the light that's like the gleam of bones. He sang the first line and we all drew back. He had told me what the phrase meant: "If I were that warrior!" and I knew by heart what came next: Enrico was going to fight for me, conquer for me, and make me the queen of his thoughts. Finally, in the song, my name appeared, and he shouted it, slow and strong and so loud I'm certain the sound woke the *orishas* in the woods, startled the animals and men who were sleeping, reached the lagoon like an arrow: Yemayá must have come up to the surface, trembling with hunger in the trembling water. It was the biggest thing that countryside had ever heard.

When he finished, Conga Mariate was crying in a very strange way. We didn't see her face, but we heard her sobbing like a little girl. I ran to a lamp and hurried to light it because I was afraid. Calazán was on his knees, his eyes rolled back, and Dominga huddled at his side like a sick bird. Enrico was sweating as he faced all of us.

"I never sang better," he said in a quiet voice.

The Congo woman walked over to him, shaking a little red handkerchief.

"You are the stallion of Changó, musyú, and his fire burns your throat."

A total of nine suspects were arrested after the explosion in the Teatro Nacional. Thirty-two years later, I was able to locate almost all of them. Some tried to deceive me, refusing to admit they had even been in the theater that afternoon, much less been arrested. Others chose to remain silent: after so many years, it was a black page that didn't seem worth remembering.

One was different: the pharmacist from El Cerro. When I went to see him he was eighty-three years old but still living in the same house he had left on that Sunday in June, in the year 1920, to attend the performance of Aïda. It was a desolate, dead house, though you could see it had once had life. I was received by one of his daughters, a woman of about fifty, who had also been at the opera that day. I didn't have the heart to lie to her; I sensed it wasn't necessary. I told her I needed to know what happened on the day the bomb exploded: it was a personal matter, something that had affected my life. She looked at me with compassion; she had deep-set eyes, and a great sadness, like a sheet of ice, lay over them. She replied that she had no information worth remembering, but her father did, and perhaps he could help me. It all depended on his state of mind: some days he spoke rationally, and on others he was like a madman. She agreed to take me to her father's room but warned me that unless he decided to talk about Caruso, I shouldn't bring the matter up.

"He spent three days in jail because of it," she said softly as we walked along a dim hallway. "It broke him, and he could never hold up his head again. One of my uncles took over the pharmacy, and my father would go there only to sit and hate. He came back with a tattoo on his hand. Say you're a nurse and take a look at his tattoo."

I told him I was a nurse. I think it was all the same to the poor ghost the pharmacist had become. He began to lecture me about magnesium bisulfate, a compound that had been popular in his day, and I took advantage of the opportunity to grasp his hand, pretending to take his pulse. I saw some words tattooed between his thumb and index finger. I had to stretch the skin to read them: JUNE 13 — FATAL AIDA. That gave me an excuse to ask about the explosion. The pharmacist became violently agitated, and his daughter came over to quiet him and signaled to me to leave them alone. I stood up to go, and that was when the old man's voice stopped me:

Wait there, listen to me: Caruso was a bandit, and other bandits from his own country followed him here. They fought their war in Havana. And just as in every other war, poor wretches like us had to pay for the damage. My pharmacy, so well-stocked . . . I had to leave it. A few hours after the explosion two policemen came here. They said my daughters and I had to go with them. I asked them what we were accused of, and they said they were arresting us because of the bomb.

They locked me up for three days, and my only crime was being at the theater that Sunday. Bracale, the impresario, told them to arrest Cubans. He knew that the people who set the bomb were foreigners, the same Sicilians who went to Matanzas afterward, trying to get Caruso. But Caruso had been hidden away by the babalawos, just imagine: he surrounded himself with blacks, he took part in their rituals, he went crazy. . . . He died a little while later.

I was happy when he died. He had fooled us all. Bracale wanted *to put on La Forza del Destino and have Caruso sing it. But Bracale didn't have rights to that opera, and a certain Señor Weber, the representative of the Ricard Company in Cuba, had all the parts confiscated. At the time, the reporter Pérez Navarro, a good friend of mine who worked for the newspaper La Noche, came to the pharmacy to buy what he always bought, Watercress Extract, so effective against influenza. Pérez Navarro looked over the parts that had been confiscated, and he told me everything: Commendatore Caruso, that extraordinary man, that marvelous singer, was a creation of the kinds of tricks that musicians find so hateful. All the numbers where the tenor appeared were marked for the maestro to transpose a tone or half tone lower than written. Even a cat could sing that way. During his appearance at the Nacional, and until the bomb carried him off to hell—or to the den of the babalawos, which amounts to the same thing—Caruso did nothing but bully the orchestra and his colleagues. I saw it with my own eyes: gesturing and keeping time with his feet and hands, imposing his rhythm on everyone else. We were horrified, myself and others who really knew opera, because in those days there were many refined amateurs. Don't think Havana was always the barnyard of ignoramuses it is now.*

I lost the pharmacy, you see. I was totally demoralized, defeated by the injustice that was done to me. It's true I carried a package into the performance, and people who saw me with that package thought it had something to do with the bomb. But all it contained were some bottles of Tonikol that I planned to deliver when I left the theater. Maybe I looked nervous—my nerves were not good because my wife had recently died. I have another daughter, who was ruined by the explosion. Lucila, the younger one, had a baby whose father was a sailor. He was one of the people arrested; he was half Italian, that's how they met, otherwise they would never have laid eyes on each other. I don't know if the sailor set the bomb; all I know is that the men who did were Caruso's pals. A war between pals.

Pérez Navarro came back afterward to buy Watercress Extract;
it was the only thing he ever bought. My brother waited on him
because I had left the pharmacy. Then he came to see me and sat
down to talk and was sorry to see me so low. "Sir, this is a
calamity," I remember him saying. "Was it really necessary to bring
that clown to Cuba?"

He told me the paper had received reports that the great tenor
was involved with a woman who was half Chinese and half mulatta,
and if that wasn't bad enough, she was a santera too. When the
bomb exploded, Caruso ran out of the theater and didn't care if the
soprano was injured or if his colleagues needed help. He didn't stop
until he reached the Parque Central; he was seen there, gasping for
breath and all dressed up as Radamès. Then he went to the Hotel
Sevilla and locked himself in his room. But the same Sicilians went
on the prowl again, and he had to get out fast. Between the two of
them—Zirato, who was his secretary, and this Bracale, who was a
real shark—they got him to Matanzas, to the house of some cabaret
performer. That's where the great Caruso hid out, with a pack of
ñáñigos protecting him, and that woman, with her Chinese snares.
Just imagine.

Besides paying high prices that day for the worst seats in the
house, up in the gallery boxes, we paid with grief for the rest of our
lives. For Caruso it was an adventure, but for us it was like falling
into a pit, a page that's suddenly turned and nothing's ever the same
again. That's what happened to my Lucila. . . . Her husband
insisted on calling the boy Verdi, and Verdi's the name they gave
him. Lucila could have made a better marriage, but the bomb turned
our lives around. The sailor disappeared—what else could you
expect?—and Verdi, that boy who was born because of the bomb,
turned out pretty bad. I can tell you that my poor Lucila is a ruined
woman. She lives in this house, but her skin became blotched and
she won't let visitors see her. As for Señor Verdi, he's a famous

crook who does his dirty work in one of those districts, San Isidro I think it is, living like a prince, my grandson, because crooks never lack for anything. Except maybe decency, but that's not his fault, it's his father's. With a name like Verdi, all he could have been was a crook, not even a baritone.

I curse the day Caruso came to Cuba. What happened in Matanzas must have cost him dear; that Chinese witchcraft tied him up in knots they say not even God could untie. He died not long afterward in New York: they say he rotted away inside. He had a young wife, but women were always his undoing. Go see Pérez Navarro, ask him, he knows more than I do about all this.

That bomb caused so much misery, that bomb destroyed our lives.

Amor fatal . . .

*I*t was the middle of the night when I woke Enrico, I brought him his cup of café con leche and gave him the message from Calazán: before daybreak we would all go to the Lagoon of San Joaquín. He lit a cigarette and complained about the heat, he grumbled that he was tired of hiding and the only thing he wanted was to leave Cuba and go back to Naples. He wasn't even interested in returning to New York, because while he was in Cuba he'd been told he would have to vacate the apartment where he'd lived for many years. For him, being forced to move was an evil omen. Enrico said that something terrible was going to happen to him, and maybe it would happen in New York. But whatever the thing was, he wanted to meet his end in Naples.

I longed to comfort him, tell him that the omen was a lie, but something made me keep quiet, a pain that gnawed at me inside, the feeling that Calazán was right: nothing could save Enrico now, and if I stayed with him I was doomed to go down too. Everything my godfather was doing, with the help of my mother and Yuan Pei Fu, the Chinaman who seemed to be my real father, was meant to keep me in Cuba and reverse what was written. Calazán was making a sacrifice by trying to change my path, he was facing the *orishas* because of me, struggling with them to protect me. He might have to pay a high price for that sacrifice, that's why he had made *Ossode* and thrown the *ékuele* for himself, to find out if the saints were very angry, or very hungry, or very stubborn about things not going the way they had ordered.

Enrico saw that I was unhappy and promised me again that I would go with him to Italy. I tried to smile, but I'm sure my smile was one more sign of fear. I took hold of his feet, I stroked his toes one by one, I confessed it had all started there, the place the Chinese *babalawos* said was the tail of the soul. His feet were the first thing I noticed when we met in the kitchen of the Hotel Inglaterra: his white feet inside Radamès' sandals. He laughed and said he hardly remembered anything about that afternoon, it seemed like centuries since the moment when he heard the explosion, ran out onto the street and into the first open door he could find. At first he hadn't even noticed I was there. Only later, when I offered to take him to a safe place, that's when he paid attention to my hair, that's when he liked my eyes. He'd never had a Chinese woman in his life, and he'd never had a mulatta. He'd like to know how a child of ours would turn out, he said, and he kissed me on the ear. When I heard that, I moved the cup of coffee away and lay down beside him. I said we should make a baby, but we had to do it thinking about the child's face. A face that wasn't mulatta or Chinese and didn't look like my face or his. He asked why I wanted a child that didn't look like us, and I told him I wanted the baby different from us so it wouldn't gather in any harm, any of the bad things that had happened or might happen to us.

"Whatever you want," Enrico whispered, putting his arms around me.

He smelled of the soaps that Zirato brought him, but his tongue had the bitter taste of the cigarettes he smoked, a taste that stayed in my throat for a long time. Years later, little drops of that bitterness would still fill my mouth, but I welcomed them, tried to hold on to them: they were the little I had left of him, what helped me most to remember.

Enrico lay so heavy on me that day, I felt him so much inside me, that at one point the memory of Baldomero came to me. I tried to chase the memory away, and I opened my eyes. I saw that Enrico's eyes were already open: "Think about the baby's face now," I said. And then I saw the face myself, not the face of a man or a woman, just a face, it might have belonged to an *orisha*, or to a spirit who wants to live, who's asking for a body, asking us to open our veins so he can mix there with our blood. Enrico gushed in me like a fish; he was dripping with sweat and his wet skin slid along mine, making the sound the waves make when they slap against the sides of a boat. I was the boat he was filling with live fish. I began to cry out with the caress of the fish, and Enrico put his hand over my mouth. I began to sob, and he kissed my eyes. Beads of sweat from his neck rolled along my throat and my breasts, like rain falling in the space between: a storm that came pushing us out of the sea and sooner or later would lead us back to the sea.

Conga Mariate, who was outside the house, shouted for us. I threw on my clothes and left Enrico as he was getting dressed, all in white, just as my godfather had instructed. When I went out, the Congo woman came toward me, lighting her way with a lantern.

"We must be at the lagoon before the sun is hot. Didn't your godfather say we had to leave at night?"

I lowered my head, I couldn't look her in the eye. The Congo woman gave me her lantern and went to stand with Calazán and Dominga. Then Enrico came out, and we all started walking along a path through the sugarcane. Whenever a rooster crowed, the Congo woman stopped and whispered words in the Lucumi language, and sometimes she touched the ground with her forehead. Day was beginning to break and Calazán walked faster, and then suddenly we saw other lights, a group of men and women waiting for us by the railroad track.

Calazán embraced the men—some of them were carrying chickens, others had ducks and white pigeons—while Enrico and I stood to one side holding hands. Conga Mariate came toward me and pulled the lantern away to put it out. It wasn't till she put it out that she thought of speaking to Enrico.

"How did the musyú sleep, how did the throat of Changó sleep?"

Enrico said he had slept well, and the Congo woman gave me a sly look, but just then the others stopped talking because Dominga stepped forward and shook the *acheré*, that's a little maraca for calling the saints. My godfather held a coconut in his hands and showed it to the four directions, then he opened the coconut and poured the water onto the track, and then one of the women handed him a gourd full of honey that he began to smear on the rails.

"Train tracks are the legs of Oggún," mumbled Conga Mariate, and she straightened her turban. "With them he walks the world."

One of the men in the group began to snort and stamp the ground. Two others came over and pulled him into the cane, they kept him hidden for a few minutes and when they brought him back he was changed: he wasn't wearing his shirt, he had his pants rolled up to his knees and a purple handkerchief on his head. Somebody offered him a cigar and he asked them to bring a light, he shouted "Fire!" and when they tried to give it to him he began to jump all around. And then he landed right beside us. Enrico stepped back, but the Congo woman spoke to him:

"Good morning, Oggún, how well you look."

The man said words in the old language and held out his hand, and the Congo woman dropped two coins into his palm. Enrico was sweating and asked if it was much farther to the lagoon. I told him it had to be very close because Calazán was going to start the killing. We both looked at the black rooster that one of the women had placed in my godfather's hands, and Enrico gave a little start when he saw how fast Calazán tore off its head.

"I am not worthy to kill," Calazán shouted. "It is Oggún who kills."

The man with the purple handkerchief threw himself to the ground and opened his mouth to receive the blood spurting from the animal's neck. He caught the blood in his hands and smeared it on his face and hair. I felt Enrico growing impatient; I stroked his back, and he looked at me without saying a word.

Finally, Calazán made his way to the head of the group. There were about fifteen of us, all dressed in white, though some of the women wore blue turbans. At a turn in the path, beyond some trees, we saw the gleam of the water. I saw it first and told Enrico. He took out his handkerchief and wiped his forehead, then he noticed how much I was sweating and tried to wipe my face, slowly he passed his handkerchief along my cheeks. I closed my eyes and breathed in his scent, and it was like breathing in poison: I felt a stabbing pain in my throat and a fiery heat coming up from my chest. I began to stagger, everything around me disappeared except for the face of Conga Mariate, she was wetting my forehead and saying words that she repeated over and over again until I closed my eyes: *"Yemayá atará . . . Iyá mio Olokún."* The pain in my throat grew stronger and stronger, and maybe that's why I forgot about Enrico, and Calazán, and the Congo woman who was fanning me, I forgot about myself and started running to the shore. Later they told me I tried to throw myself headfirst into a muddy corner of the lagoon; I grabbed a black duck away from a woman who was washing it for the sacrifice and I went into the water with that duck and passed out. When I came to, the man in the purple handkerchief was beside me, blowing the smoke from his mouth at me, smiling at me with his black face, a face I had seen in dreams. I knew I was coming out of a trance, that Yemayá had "mounted" me and commanded me to carry her to the water. Behind me two black women were struggling to twist a tortoise's neck. The animal kept fighting, kept trying to hide in its shell, until another black woman, the oldest one of all, came and bent her finger like a hook and put it inside and pulled out the tortoise's head. Before I knew it, the head had been cut off and somebody was catching all the blood in a little jug. They helped me up, they wet my lips with the tortoise blood and sprinkled my face with rum. That was when I felt strong enough to look for Enrico. I tried to see over the group, and in the distance I could hear the voice of Conga Mariate: *"Yemayá atará . . . Iyá mio Olokün."* I was desperate when I didn't see him, and I dared to ask Calazán about him:

"Where did you take him?"

"Bite your tongue," my godfather answered. "Respect the saints."

My mouth filled with water, the lagoon water that I had swallowed while I was "mounted." I vomited on the grass, and Dominga came and held my head.

"Have you seen Enrico?"

She pointed at the cane.

"They're undressing him. They'll take him to the lagoon to change his life."

In those days I had long black hair that hung below my waist. It was very straight hair: I must have gotten it from my father no matter who my father was, Noro Cheng or Yuan Pei Fu. With my hair streaming water I ran to Enrico, who came out of the cane naked—all he had on were his white shoes and a sheet around his shoulders. Behind him walked Conga Mariate and some other women who were chanting and looking down at the ground. Our eyes met. The sun was already high and the light was unbearable, like a flash of lightning that didn't move from that mysterious point, the terror of heaven. The Congo woman gestured for me to keep my distance, and Enrico looked at me again, like a little child torn from his mother's arms, like an animal being led to sacrifice. I made a move to go to him, and Calazán grabbed my arm:

"Don't you dare, damn it."

Some of the blacks surrounded Enrico, and a few began to sing. The Congo woman seemed to be the leader: she was the one who began each phrase and the others listened and repeated her dark song. Calazán walked to the group, he made his way to Enrico and placed a hand on his shoulder. He obliged him to kneel before the water, he pushed down his head until his forehead touched the ground, and then he began to talk about him to the *orishas*. "He is also your child," was all I could understand, all he kept repeating, until finally he told Enrico to stand and take off his shoes, to take off the sheet and close his eyes. Somebody handed a white duck to my godfather, and my godfather passed it over Enrico's body, always moving down: from his shoulders to his hands, from his neck to his privates, from his waist to his feet. When he was finished with that mortal body he tossed the living duck into the water. The animal sank but surfaced right away, it shook itself and stayed there, floating all alone. Then a woman stepped forward with a basket of pigeons. She threw them one by one into the water, and they all disappeared, swept away by the current.

My godfather made a sign to Enrico to go into the lagoon. I was surprised when Enrico obeyed without a word, not turning around or even trying to look at me. He walked into the water and nobody followed him; the men stood watching and the Congo woman stopped singing. He had told me he was a good swimmer, he'd been swimming since he was little, and when the water came up to his chest I thought he would swim back to shore. But instead he kept walking, not moving his arms, going deeper and deeper until the water came up to his chin.

I looked at Calazán and at Conga Mariate, and had a premonition they were both waiting for Enrico to go all the way under. I felt the stabbing in my throat again, my whole body shuddered with pain: it was my life, not Enrico's, that was changing at the bottom of the lagoon. I leaped toward the water and called him, but he didn't react, he was rigid, and Calazán gave me an angry look. I called him again and then I broke into a run, nobody dared to stop me, I ran like a crazy woman into the water. The most amazing thing was the silence, the only sound was my voice, my voice screaming: "Enrico! Enrico!"

His head went under just as I reached him. I never imagined I could lift a man into the air. All I know is that I held him up and my arms turned into the arms of the lagoon. I screamed at him to take his head out of the water and he did: Enrico came out of the water with his eyes open, with eyes I didn't recognize. I dragged him to shore and saw two men coming to help me, and Conga Mariate came too, she was carrying a blanket that she put around his shoulders. Enrico was coughing and had to lean on the black men's arms to walk. Calazán was waiting for him with a little glass of rum.

"Drink; it's the impression left by the water."

He took a sip, shook his head, then drank it down in one swallow. Conga Mariate began to sing: she was the leader and the others followed her song. Calazán sent Dominga to wrap me in a blanket too.

"Yemayá is a queen who knows many secrets," she said in a

low voice, wiping the mud from my face, "but she bows in reverence to King Changó."

I went to stand beside Enrico and asked him if he was cold. It was a stupid question because we were all panting with the heat. We took each other's hand, and I could see his lips trembling. He was saying goodbye, with his mind and his eyes he was saying goodbye to me. Tears came to my eyes, I was sure Enrico had seen everything when he lowered his head into the lagoon. That's why he had come out with his eyes open, that's why he was so changed. Now he had no doubts, and I couldn't have doubts either. In the currents at the bottom he had seen his life, his homeland in Naples, his dead mother and father, and his own throat, the flame that the water of death would soon put out. In the lagoon he had seen his end, and in my trance I had seen it too. We held each other in terror, we pressed our bodies together because we were alone. Nobody was looking at us now, the black men and women didn't care about us anymore, we didn't matter to my godfather, or Dominga, or Conga Mariate, who was busy wrapping yarrow leaves around the neck of a duck whose eyes she had also covered with the leaves.

"*Yemayá fumi ibá le bi so lo*," shouted one of the black women.

There was the sound of bells, *agogó* is what those little bells are called; they move by themselves and make our skin crawl. I sobbed against Enrico's chest. He seemed resigned, he kept looking at the struggling bird, and he didn't jump back, he didn't close his eyes, he didn't move a single muscle when Conga Mariate tore off the animal's head with her teeth.

"*Owó Yemayá fumi lo owó*," Calazán wailed, he had changed into something so black and unreal, into a bird that looked like a nightjar, its voice damaged by a brightness it could not bear.

My head was burning, and I felt cool hands take me by the

shoulders and move me away from Enrico. It was the oldest woman, the one who had caught the tortoise's head with the hook of her finger. When I turned around, she kneeled down in front of me and tried to kiss my feet.

"Lady, Lady Kediké."

My godfather had told me that Lady Kediké was one of the many names of the Yemayá of the lagoon. The old woman stood up, smiling, and put her arms around my waist.

"*Omó te mi,*" she said. She repeated it a few times and looked at Enrico out of the corner of her eye. Then she walked away and went to dance with the rest of the women, all of them happy with the smell of the yarrow mixed with the smell of rum and the smell of blood and the smell of the candles burning along the shore.

Conga Matiate, who was following the position of the sun, shouted something in Lucumi, telling all the women to stop dancing. It was twelve noon: the most dangerous time of day, the hour when the evil spirits of the world rose up and you had to lift your feet, if you could, and make the sign of the cross in the name of God. A man walked toward us, twirling a guinea hen. I knew the ceremony was about to end.

"We will meet our obligations," Calazán insisted.

It was the last sacrifice: a drop of blood for each *orisha*. The body of the guinea hen was still quivering on the ground when I went over to dip my fingers. It was what I had seen my mother do ever since I was a little girl, what I had seen my godfather do. With my fingers smeared in blood, I crossed myself.

Dominga, who didn't take her eyes off us, brought Enrico's shoes and shirt. He had put on his trousers but still had the blanket over his shoulders. I kneeled down, cleaned the mud from his feet and put them into his shoes, I tied the laces for him as though he really was my king. Enrico asked if it was all over.

"We've met our obligations to the lagoon," Dominga answered, imitating the way Calazán talked, "but tomorrow we must come back to give thanks to Olokún and receive his *aché*.

I thought Enrico was going to be sulky or sad, but it was just the opposite, he seemed more peaceful. On the way back he asked me what the *aché* was and I said it was the blessing, the strong skill, the craft the *orishas* gave to each person. Calazán acted very proud, he was distant with us. It was after two when we came to the house. From the distance we saw a car in front of the gate and Enrico became excited because he knew right away it was his secretary. I felt scared, I was always afraid they would come and take him away. Zirato was there, waiting for us at the entrance, but he walked toward us and hugged Enrico and then he shook my hand. I could tell by his eyes he was surprised to see that we were wet, that Enrico was sunburned. The two of them went into the house, talking in Italian, and I followed my godfather, I followed him to the kitchen, where Conga Mariate began to put away some herbs and Dominga was starting to cook a chicken.

"Why did you push him into the water?"

The Congo woman dropped the herbs and Dominga stepped back from the pot. They stared at me but Calazán didn't even bother to look at me.

"I'm talking to you, Godfather: why did you push him into the lagoon?"

He raised his head, and the look he gave me didn't seem angry or annoyed. It was a look of pity.

"I could turn your face inside out if I wanted to. I won't do it because you're crazy, your Eledá has had too much sun."

My Eledá was my guardian angel, the spirit who lives in my head and should never get too heated up.

"Why did you want him to drown?"

"I didn't know it at first," my godfather answered slowly, "but now I've seen what I had to see. Do you know how he's going to die? I'll tell you: he'll die howling like an animal, his screams will be heard night and day, he's going to suffer a great deal before he leaves this world, and when the final moment comes, a black stink, the breath of Ikú, will rise from his whole body. That stink will drive him crazy. The people at his side will want to run away because they won't be able to stand the smell. Just think, Aida, you lost the chance to let him die in peace."

I burst into tears, but the Congo woman came and slapped me in the face.

"Shame on you. Respect the will of the *orishas*, or don't you even respect them?"

"She's a paisana," Dominga murmured in a scornful voice. "They only respect Sanfancón."

Those words, that reminder, acted like a tranquilizer. I dried my tears and looked at Calazán:

"Forgive me, Godfather."

He turned his back, and I went into Enrico's room. I saw Zirato packing his suitcase, while Enrico sat next to the window and smoked.

"We're leaving for Santa Clara."

Zirato stopped, as though it surprised him that Enrico had told me.

All Enrico had to do was give him a look:

"She's coming with us."

I began to get my things together—there wasn't much. Zirato went out to put the suitcase in the car, and Enrico asked me to give him my hand. I held out my hand and he turned it over, palm up. He took something shiny from his pocket, a gold nugget the size of an egg. Set into the gold was a sliver of wood, and next to the wood was a little plaque with words engraved on it. He read the words, he said them first in Italian and I couldn't understand; but he said them again while he put the nugget in my hand.

I felt its weight and brought it up to my eyes, I turned it around slowly so I could see all of it, I stroked my cheeks with it. Finally, I kissed the plaque and the little piece of wood he'd had them pull from the rubble.

"In memory of the bomb that made us burn," he whispered in words I could understand, and he closed my fingers over it.

I put my arms around him, fell to my knees, leaned my head against his belly, my mouth against his privates, against everything I loved best, everything it hurt me to lose. We could hear singing from the kitchen. It was the voice of Conga Mariate singing a slave song, something distant and mournful, like the grieving seed of the *orisha* it was dedicated to. I was so crazy I thought I heard Dominga's voice too:

"Yemayá is a queen who knows many secrets, but she bows in reverence to King Changó."

My secrets weren't worth anything, they couldn't save us. But my reverence could, and maybe my love. We could die now, everything on this earth was over for us. The voice of the Congo woman grew stronger, sounded nearer:

"*Immense Olofi, spirit of the world.*"

Enrico took me by the arms and made me stand up.

"*Immense Olofi . . . we invoke you, we invoke you.*"

His hand clutched at my hair, his tongue licked my face. I thought he was going to say he loved me, but he said something else:

"It's true," was all he said. "It's true."

*W*hen I met him, Vicente Pérez Navarro was living with half a body and half a soul. I went to his house in Vedado afraid we wouldn't be able to talk at all. I had been told he was very sick, he was paralyzed and with almost no voice. His wife was happy to see me. She said that visitors cheered him up, and she took me to her husband's studio, a room filled with recordings and opera mementos. The largest photograph on the wall, the one that stood out, was of a dark man wearing a linen suit and a Panama hat. The dedication read: TO MY DEAR FRIEND PÉREZ NAVARRO, WITH THE AFFECTION OF HIPÓLITO LÁZARO, MONTEVIDEO, 1915.

There was also a photograph of a group of men and women crowding around a street lamp in the Parque Central. I went up to it to read: FOR PÉREZ NAVARRO, THE INSPIRATION AND GUIDE OF HIS FRIENDS IN THE COMPANY PAYRET.

Behind me I heard a rasping voice say, "Good afternoon." It was Pérez Navarro; his wife was pushing him in a wheelchair. The left side of his body did not exist: the eye and arm were immobile, half of his lopsided smile was frozen. I walked to him and shook his right hand, the only one he could move, a defeated hand, like the neck of a wounded bird. His wife brought me a chair and placed it beside him, and I repeated the lie I had told him on the phone: I was a student at the university, taking courses in art history, and in the afternoon I assisted a professor who was planning to write a book about Caruso.

"What's this professor's name?" Pérez Navarro asked.

I gave him the first name that came to mind, an unknown actor who had just started at the Blue Network.

"Eduardo Egea," I said.

"I don't know him," murmured Pérez Navarro, and he asked his wife to bring him the letter. She went straight to the desk and took a paper out of a folder, examined it front and back, and handed it, with great distaste, to her husband.

"I want to read you something," he said in a very clear voice. I realized that his hoarseness occasionally disappeared, and then his true voice could be heard, a deep voice that didn't sound particularly old. But this wouldn't last very long, and in a few minutes he became tongue-tied again, the rest of his words trapped in his throat. Then his voice became raspy, as hoarse and ragged as before.

"'My esteemed friend,'" he read slowly. "'This afternoon, on the steamship Cartago, I will leave Havana, sincerely gratified by the kindness of its citizens, who have my undying admiration. I will always remember the attentiveness and courtesy of the Cuban people, who should be proud to live in the most beautiful country in the Atlantic. My heart is full of gratitude to those who favored me with their applause and praise. I beg you to find room in your distinguished newspaper for this farewell message. With my respectful greetings to the Havana press, I am, most sincerely yours, Enrico Caruso.'"

Pérez Navarro attempted to sustain his voice but couldn't; it was as if the mere mention of that name, Enrico Caruso, strangled him. He coughed twice and turned livid. His wife brought him a cup that was on the end table, I believe he took a few sips of an orange tea, and as he drank he looked into my eyes.

"He didn't send that letter to me," he said with a sigh, gesturing for me to take the paper. "He couldn't stand the sight of me. He sent it to the editor of El Mundo. Naturally the paper published it, and later a reporter, a friend of mine, took it from the files and gave it to me as a kind of joke: he knew what I thought of Caruso; he knew I was one person, at least, Caruso couldn't fool."

I bent my head and inspected the sheet of yellowing paper, frayed along the edges. Pérez Navarro began to cough again, and I looked at Caruso's signature. It was the first time I had seen his handwriting, and I felt an emotion I hadn't anticipated, as if instead of seeing his writing I was hearing his voice for the first time, a voice that kept repeating certain words to me: "Atlantic . . . farewell . . . heart."

"The case of the bomb was never solved," said Pérez Navarro, and he gestured again for me to return the letter.

Mario García Kohly, the Cuban ambassador to Spain, told reporters in Madrid that some anarchists who had been expelled from the Republic had ordered the theater blown up. No one believed him, of course. Two days after the explosion, a stagehand came to see me at the paper and swore he had information more explosive than the bomb. We went to a nearby bar, where he told me that the device had been placed by Caruso himself, not personally but by one of his servants, a man named Punzo. At one time this Punzo had been a singer, the favorite pupil of Vergine, who was Caruso's teacher as well. Vergine had placed all his hopes in Punzo, who happened to be an extremely vain man. Vergine accepted Caruso as a student because he owed a favor to a mutual friend of theirs, a wealthy baritone named Missiano, who had asked him to take Caruso on and even paid for his lessons. Years later Caruso happened to run into Punzo, who never made his mark as a singer, and Punzo asked him for a job. Caruso hired him as his valet; that was his revenge. To make matters worse, I don't know if he ordered him to set the bomb. But ask yourself this: Was an explosion beneficial to Enrico Caruso? On one hand, yes, because the reporters forgot about his fakery, forgot about his decline as a singer. On the other hand, no, because his dirty dealings might have come to light, all his crooked Neapolitan tricks. The same day the bomb went off, his American wife reported to the police that her jewelry had been stolen. Some said the robbery was staged. Caruso refused to allow the police to dig up the area around his house in East Hampton where people said the jewels were hidden, and the insurance company threatened not to pay. It's my understanding they never did. That's how the great tenor spent his final days: this was the wake left behind by his glory.

We stopped for a while. I was writing at a good pace; it was easy to follow him because he spoke so slowly. His wife asked if I'd like coffee or lemonade. I told her lemonade just as Pérez Navarro mumbled something about Bruno Zirato. I leaned forward in my seat and asked him to repeat it:

I said that I had a serious confrontation with Zirato, Caruso's secretary. One morning I went to the Hotel Sevilla—I always went there for coffee—and happened to see a group of reporters from the Diario de la Marina who asked me to join them at their table. Zirato was at the table, too, and when he heard my name his face changed color, and to be sure he asked if I was the Pérez Navarro who worked on La Noche, and when I replied "your servant," he said I was servant only to the Company Payret and the exquisite Hipólito Lázaro. His tone was sarcastic when he said "exquisite." Caruso blamed the coldness of Cuban audiences on Lázaro's fans.

I stood and felt someone take my arm. I tried to slap Zirato, who also got to his feet and took a step back. This happened five or six days after the explosion. In Havana there was a good deal of talk about where Caruso could be, and I had written an article, giving it a comic twist: RADAMÈS AND MADAMA, WHERE ARE THE BUTTERFLIES HIDING? The article had a good amount of metaphor and double entendre. But everybody knew it was about Caruso and his girlfriend, who turned out to be half Chinese. And that was another of the rumors circulating about the bomb, the most delicate, the one that all the reporters kept quiet about: somebody had wanted to get rid of him over a woman. This Chinese girl, who was also half mulatta, had been involved with the owner of an opium den. Later on, I went by there quite a few times to see if I could find out anything, and some Chinamen were living in that house, all crowded together the way those people live, and the one who guarded it, armed with razors, was a cripple. One day I saw that the door was open, and I offered the cripple a cigarette and he gave me a little paper lantern; he pretended that he used the razors for cutting paper and not for slicing up intruders, which is what he really did.

I couldn't see Caruso's girlfriend then, but I got to meet her later, in the most unexpected place, at the most unexpected time. It was about two years after the bomb went off, maybe a little longer, because Caruso had been dead for some time. I was in a tavern on Reina Boulevard, a place called La Flor de Reina, and I had ordered some oysters. I'm mentioning the oysters because I remember I had just put one in my mouth when one of the men tending bar stopped and stared out at the street: "What a looker," he said to a friend. "She's the Chink who hid Caruso."

I turned and saw a woman from the back. She had Chinese hair, dark and straight, but her body was a mulatta's. I'm too old to explain to you why it was a mulatta's body, I'll just say it had the spark. I was out of there like a shot; my intention was not to talk to her but just to look, to see her face. When I was next to her I said "Excuse me, Señora," and she lifted her head and looked at me. She wasn't a girl, she was thirty or more, and she had the eyes of a Filipina Chinese and a nose that could pass for white. But her mouth was something divine. It wasn't black or Chinese. It was the mouth of Mary Maclaren, an actress I was very fond of in those days. In my heart I cursed Caruso: he'd swindled us out of thousands of dollars and on top of that he was lucky enough to get this incredible woman. I didn't say anything, and she kept walking. I didn't try to stop her, not at all. I went back into the tavern. The bartender had seen everything, seen me go out to look at her, seen me left speechless.

I asked him to tell me the story about Caruso. He shrugged and said he really didn't know anything, just the dumb things people say. I took out a five-peso bill and put it on the bar: 'Tell me, compadre.' He shook his head; really, he didn't know. I took back the five and pulled out a twenty. Twenty pesos back then was a fortune, and the man's eyes lit up. He left to get a bottle, and in a little while he came back and poured me another drink. "I used to work in the kitchen of the Hotel Inglaterra," he said in a quiet voice. "I was working there when the bomb went off." Then he told me that the woman we had just seen was a good friend of the cook's and would stop in the kitchen of the Inglaterra to wait for Caruso, who came for her almost every night, incognito, in a blue Packard. They had known each other for a while, ever since Caruso arrived in Cuba, or maybe even longer, who knows, but on the day of the bomb it all came out in the open, people knew about his Chinese girlfriend because Caruso ran from the theater and the only thing he could think of was to hide in the Inglaterra, crawl under the skirts of the woman who was already there waiting for him. The bartender said that he was peeling vegetables and washing dishes, and the cook, who was his boss, sent him to find a cab. As soon as the cab came, Caruso and the woman disappeared. "The two of them left," he said, "that delicious Chinita and the fat man dressed up like a mandarin." He told me a reporter was at the Inglaterra the next day, asking if it was true that the great Caruso had been there. But the cook had warned him not to open his mouth. "And now I'm finally opening it," he said with a laugh, and added this: he had seen her afterward with a belly, about six months pregnant, and he bet Caruso had left her that little present.

That's the information I got for my twenty pesos. I planned to use it all in an article and even suggest that the Chinamen at the opium den might have been behind the explosion, but the editor, who was a good friend of mine, said: "Pérez Navarro, compadre, you're obsessed with Caruso. Let the dead rest in peace and don't get involved with those Chinamen: they're from California and they'll slit your throat." I thought it over and I forgot about that Chinese girl, or mulatta, or whatever she was. She's probably dead by now, and if she hasn't died

she must be pretty old, how old do you think she is? Sixty? And you,
my girl, how old are you? Thirty, thirty-one . . . ?

Pérez Navarro smiled, and I didn't look away. His wife brought
me a glass of lemonade and I hid my agitation by drinking very
slowly. Before I left I gave him my address and a false last name,
because he told me there were details he couldn't recall for the
moment, but he'd dictate them to his wife as he thought of them, and
then mail them to me.

A few months later I received a thick envelope addressed to
Enriqueta Cheng, my real name, and not to Enriqueta Gómez, the
name I had given him. Inside the envelope was a letter from Pérez
Navarro's wife, informing me of his death. There was also the
farewell letter written by Enrico Caruso. And, finally, a strange note
dictated by Pérez Navarro himself. I shivered as I read it. I felt pity,
and then fear. By the end, I was crying:

My dear Enriqueta,

You are the best part of the bomb: the dust suspended in
midair, the great, momentary hush, all that confusion pierced
by light. Even the most repellent actions have their hidden
good. I am leaving you your father's letter. He would feel proud
if he could see you: you look exactly like him, the same chin
and nose, and a vague resemblance around those eyes, which
are somewhat Chinese but Neapolitan as well. I didn't have a
moment's doubt, I knew who you were from the beginning,
and still I told you the truth, I told you what I knew, I didn't
hold back a single word, good or bad. Forgive me,

—Pérez Navarro

I kept the letter and told my mother about it. By this time she was
bedridden, and her condition was grave. She gave an uneasy sigh.

"I remember that man," she said. "I remember the day he stopped me on the street."

I asked her if it was true that I looked like Caruso.

"You look like him," she said, touching her finger to my chin. "You have that little dimple here; he had it too."

She took away her finger and laid her hand along my cheek, then she said "Enrico." It was the first, the only time I saw her weep for him, weep in that bitter way, with cries and moans. I asked her please to calm down, and she said she couldn't help it because she was seeing him. She went into a kind of trance, I was afraid she was dying. I sat with her for hours, and for all those hours she simply repeated this phrase over and over:

"Goodbye, earth, goodbye."

Presago il core . . .

I'm in Signa, my house in Signa, arranging a crèche and humming an aria from *Manon*. Bruno Bruni is playing the same melody on the piano. It's hot but the wind bothers me. I'm going to tell them to close the window, and then I see you there, sitting there, next to the portrait of my mother. I want to ask you when you arrived, but Bruno plays louder and my words can't be heard. I get up, and the figures from the crèche start to fly in front of me. I can't see you anymore, I can't see Bruno, I can't even hear the music. And a voice, I think it's my father's voice, says: 'Rico, at last you've died.'"

It was the first night in Santa Clara. Enrico woke up trembling, complaining he couldn't breathe. I said he must have had a bad dream, and he said it hadn't been good or bad, but something he couldn't understand. Then he began to tell me the dream; it made me afraid, but I let him talk. He said that something like the dream happened last summer, in his house in Signa. Bruno Bruni was at the piano, and Enrico was humming the melody while he cleaned a crèche. Suddenly there was a gust of wind, a strong wind that blew some of the figures over. He got up to close the window and heard somebody out there talking to him. It was a feeling in his soul, because nobody was there. Just that brilliant sky, without any clouds, the August sky over Signa. The pianist stopped playing and asked what was wrong, and Enrico said he didn't know, but somebody was trying to tell him something.

"Now somebody's trying to tell me something again," he said.

I got up to find some towels. I dried his body and put wet cloths on his forehead. I asked him to dream something nicer, and he promised he'd dream about Del Pezzo's, it was his favorite restaurant. He laughed when he said it, but it was a dying laugh, the kind of laugh that can break between your lips like dark, dangerous glass. He finally dozed off, and that's when I knew that from then on I'd be the one who wouldn't be able to sleep. I started to think about what would happen if he got sick again, if he felt the same pain he'd felt in Regla. Calazán wasn't in Santa Clara, neither was Conga Mariate or even Dominga, and I wouldn't know what to do on my own.

Zirato seemed very strange to me. A skinny, mysterious man who looked at me as if he thought I was mysterious too. The house where we were staying in Santa Clara wasn't a place that made you feel happy or peaceful. Just the opposite: it felt to me like a house where there'd been a lot of suffering. My mother always said that the crying you do inside sticks to the furniture like soot, and after a while you breathe it back in, you breathe in the sorrow that turns into smoke. That's why when she cried, and she didn't cry very often, she would run out of the house and lean against a tree. She told me to do the same thing, but there were days when I felt so much sadness I didn't have the strength to get up and walk, to go outside and cry. That's how it was when my little girl died, and that's how it must have been for the people who lived in that house in Santa Clara: they cried their hearts out indoors, they didn't have the strength to stand up. And there we were, trying to sleep in a room where you breathed in grief, breathed in sorrow that was like perfume: it passed back and forth across my face, it came in my nostrils and weighed heavy on my chest.

A little while before we left Matanzas, José de Calazán took me aside, put a hand on my shoulder, and gave me a father's look: "What can we do for you, Aida?" I thought about it; you had to think very carefully about the answers you gave my godfather. I was tempted to say: "Don't do anything for me, do it for him." But I was afraid to provoke him again. I had already provoked him enough by being crazy and deciding to follow Enrico to Santa Clara. I answered with what I thought was the easiest thing to do:

"Let my mother know I'm all right, and the only way I'll be better is if I stay with Enrico."

Calazán's eyes clouded over: "Then nothing can be done for you now."

Conga Mariate handed me a basket with fruit and slices of bread for the train. Dominga reminded her that on modern trains they served meals, and they got tangled up in an argument that stopped as soon as they caught sight of Enrico dressed all in white, in a cloud of cologne. He wanted to say goodbye to Calazán first; he went over to my godfather and they talked in quiet voices and shook hands. Then he went to Dominga and gave her some bills, and when he tried to do the same with Conga Mariate she stopped him cold and made the sign of the cross over him, saying a prayer in the old language. He looked calmer and more cheerful, as though he'd come back to life, as though sinking into the water of the lagoon had roused him from a great fatigue, or a great sorrow.

But that first night in Santa Clara brought him low again. In the morning he was downhearted; he opened his eyes but couldn't, or wouldn't, get up. He smoked for a long time, staring at the ceiling, at the glass beads on the chandelier, until he finished the whole pack. Then he opened a new one and took out another cigarette, and with that cigarette dangling from his lips he jumped out of bed and went into the bathroom. I saw him stop in front of the mirror and look at himself, not moving a muscle. And he kept looking at himself as he finished the cigarette. Then he did his gargling. I heard him cough and spit, cough and spit, over and over again until his saliva came out clear. When that happened he would say something in Italian, a phrase I learned because it struck me so funny: *"Lo strumento è pulito."*

That morning in Santa Clara, he didn't say it. He came out and didn't say anything. I was the one who reminded him of the words. Enrico smiled, stroked my head, and put his arms around me, not with the desire of the body, only with the desire of the heart. A little while later Zirato came in with three men I didn't know, who had just arrived from Havana. One was Mario Fantini, the servant who took care of his clothes and the mountain of sheets they took with them wherever they went. Punzo was there too; he hardly looked at me, but Enrico had told me he took care of his costumes for the opera. Finally, I met Salvatore Fucito, the musician who helped him rehearse. A bald, thickset man with a big handlebar mustache came to the house after them. He said hello to Zirato, and Zirato introduced him to the others: he said this was the impresario Rafael de Armas, they called him "Armitas." This "Armitas" twirled the ends of his mustache while he looked at me out of the corner of his eye, and finally he looked straight at me and asked who the lady was. Zirato didn't know what to say, Mario pretended he was brushing a hat, and everybody waited to see how Enrico would react, and his reaction was fast, he took me by the arm and said: "This is Aïda."

He had a performance at the Teatro Caridad that same night, and they told Enrico reporters had come from Havana and wanted to talk to him about the bomb. I had a premonition that if I went to the theater it would cause problems, and Enrico himself proved it: before he left for rehearsal he took me aside and said he thought I should skip the performance in Santa Clara and wait for the one in Cienfuegos. That was the city we were going to next. When he saw how sad I was he made a suggestion: I ought to spend the afternoon looking around Santa Clara, and he asked me to buy him some handkerchiefs. Zirato gave me an envelope with money and told me what kind of handkerchiefs they had to be.

As soon as they left I put on my hat and went out. First I wandered for a while, with no particular direction in mind, thinking about the great adventure of my life, about everything that could happen when we got back to Havana and I'd have to say goodbye to my mother; and maybe say goodbye to Calazán, who'd be back in Regla by then, and last of all I'd say goodbye to my real father, the old man Yuan Pei Fu, a flesh-and-blood father who'd been like a dream father, always hidden behind the glare of the smoke.

I bought the handkerchiefs Enrico had asked for; they had to be exactly the size and fabric Zirato had said. Then I shopped for clothes for myself. Like any good seamstress, I never bought ready-made clothes, and that's what was really unusual about my walk: carrying parcels with skirts and blouses made me feel strange, like a vain woman. Along the way a little black boy offered to help me, but I said no because it had started to rain and I decided to go into a café until it stopped. When I walked in, I noticed that everybody was looking at me, they knew I wasn't from Santa Clara and they were trying to figure out where I came from: a Chinese mulatta was no upper-class lady, and yet they must have thought I was acting like one.

I ordered hot chocolate, and since it was really coming down outside, more and more people came into the café. The men gave their seats to the women, and the ones who came in last crowded around the tables or jostled one another at the door to watch the rain pouring down like crazy. One of the men who was standing, a young man, began to stare at me. For the whole time I could feel his eyes on my face, my hands, even the cup I was drinking from. He made me very uncomfortable, so I wiped my mouth and decided to leave even though it was still raining. He probably saw that; he knew I was getting up and he came over to the table. His style made an impression on me, the way he held his hat; he was very elegant and wore a ring with a black stone.

"Excuse me," he said, "aren't you Señora de Caruso?"

I must have turned pale because he made a move as though he wanted to keep me from falling. I looked at him for a moment and saw he had a sincere expression, but something told me not to trust him.

"I'm not that person," I said, trying to make my way through the crowd, carrying all my packages out to the flooded street. He hurried after me.

"I'm Cipriano Rivas, I'm with the *Diario de la Marina*. Don't you want to tell me how your husband is?"

I turned around and lifted my chin: "I don't know what you're talking about."

I raised my voice, and other people looked at us. The man gave a little bow, and finally I could leave. I looked back two or three times to see if he was following me, but he wasn't. It had stopped raining and the streets were getting back to normal, lots of people were riding by on horses, and I walked faster until I was lost in the crowd.

When I got to the house, with my muddy shoes and wet clothes, Enrico was already there, lying on the bed, staring at the ceiling again and smoking one cigarette after another. I told him I had bought the handkerchiefs, but I didn't have the heart to mention what had happened with the reporter. Instead, I got undressed and sat down beside him. I asked him what he thought of the theater, and his answer was that all theaters were the same to him. His voice was bitter, and I didn't say anything.

"I sing for money," he added, looking at me through the smoke.

It seemed to me he wanted to get something off his chest, I wiped the sweat from his face and kissed him behind the ear, on his hair soaked with cologne. He whispered that the only thing he still liked was drawing, and that's why he never sold his sketches. Then he took it back: he also liked looking at his crèches, those wonders that were almost alive, they were waiting for him at the Villa Bellosguardo. I put my arms around him and we were quiet for a while: with my eyes closed, I was thinking about my own ghosts, about how far away my old life, my thoughts before the bomb, seemed now. His eyes were open, seeing who knows what visions, looking at a place not of this world, a scene that came from his soul.

That night, before he left to sing, he whispered to me:

"Don't talk to anybody."

I promised I wouldn't leave the house, and I watched him go out with Zirato and Mario; Punzo and Fucito had gone ahead so they'd be the first ones at the theater. Months later I learned that the papers said Enrico was at the house of a family named Berenguer, which was really where Zirato was staying. The Berenguers were giving a dinner that night after the performance, and it must have been the first time Enrico set foot in their house, just for a few hours, until the other guests left and he could come back to his refuge, the little hiding place he was sharing with me.

I used this time to look over the clothes I'd bought. I arranged everything in a kind of trunk Zirato had brought us, and that's what I was doing when somebody knocked at the door. It was close to midnight, and I was expecting Enrico but it didn't occur to me to open the door right away, instead I went to the window to see who it was. I caught a glimpse of a shadow, a woman running away. Then I saw that she'd slipped an envelope under the door. A flat envelope addressed to Enrico Caruso. It was sealed tight, and I held it for a while, sniffed at it but didn't find out a thing, held it up to the light. When Enrico finally got back, along with Mario, who was going to spend the night with us, I handed him the envelope and told him how it had been delivered. He opened it and took out a sheet of paper that seemed very big to me for the few lines written on it. He said something in Italian to Mario, who took the paper and read it. I didn't dare to ask what it said; Enrico's face didn't invite questions. What I did do was follow him into the bedroom and help him undress; his shirt was soaked and I tossed it to one side and listened to him complain about the heat. He asked me to open the windows, but all of them were open, and I began to fan him. I fanned him with one hand and dried his neck and chest with the other. After a while he asked me if I was sure that a woman had left the envelope. I said I couldn't be sure, but that's how it looked in the dark, and then he told me that they'd threatened him again, that's what was on the paper.

"They say there's going to be another bomb," he whispered, "and in Cienfuegos they won't miss."

I didn't stop fanning him, but I felt something piercing my heart, an emptiness that was too painful, the tremor of all the omens coming at the same time, all coming together in the same place. I said I thought we should go back to Havana, and he shook his head. He looked older, and I was sure he would collapse any minute. Then he said it was all the same to him: Santa Clara, Havana, New York. . . . Finally he opened his heart and told me that while he was at the theater he'd received a cable: his butler and chauffeur in New York were in jail, they'd been arrested for conspiracy and theft.

"I don't even trust Zirato," he whispered in my ear.

I put my arms around him, and he did the same, but his arms had no strength. I could feel his wet skin, and for a moment I pictured myself like another liquid, one that came from a different kind of heat, maybe from my own fear. Enrico was alone, somebody or something was circling, closing in on him, and Calazán and I, and in a way my father, Yuan Pei Fu, were the only people in this world who knew that the circle had already closed. I could have left if I wanted to: I had the privilege of choosing, the chance to stay on the outside; that's what Calazán and my mother wanted, and maybe my father too, though my father, being so close to Sanfancón, had a clearer vision, he saw all the possible roads and knew exactly which one would be mine. In the end, I decided to stay inside, stay with Enrico and be like water, be his current, a tide that rose and fell: Yemayá bowing in reverence to King Changó.

When the bomb exploded, a piece of my life had blown away, a piece that had been lent to me and went back to the place where it belonged. Those places are mysterious, our whole life is mysterious. I didn't love Enrico the way I might have loved some other man. I know it's hard to understand, I'm just beginning to understand it now: I loved him not the way you love a person but the way you love a space, a place, a time you want back, another life that shows up in this one. It was more like death than anything else.

The next morning, while Enrico was kissing me, my mind was still going back and forth along those paths. I was trying to put my life and my feelings in order, until I couldn't think anymore because he came into me, his whole body in me, everything he had: that was really the moment you came into the world. That was the moment, Enriqueta—not the day you were conceived, not the morning in March when you were born. I was clean, I smelled sweet, I was much younger than your father, and I was so ready to receive him that he gave himself with almost no effort. He was so tired of singing, he was sweating, he was suffering, and only my hands knew how to bring him relief.

I remember that the paper with the threat lay forgotten in the sheets, and I remember that I pulled it out, many hours later, and it was wet, it had turned into something dark and blurred.

Late that night, we left for Cienfuegos.

*O*n the second of August, 1952, my mother and I sat in front of the photograph of Enrico Caruso. The night before we had lit a candle for him and burned incense. In this picture, he was a man in a dark hat, with thin lips that didn't look as if they could sing, and a pair of black eyes that no one would have guessed were about to close forever. The photograph was taken in Sorrento, just a few days before his death. My mother received it a year later, along with some money. She never knew who sent the envelope; it contained only the photograph and the bills.

"Your father has been dead thirty-one years today," she said, taking my hands.

I knew she was reaching the end of her story, the story she was telling me and also the story of her own life: she was feeling weaker and weaker, perhaps because of her sickness, but especially because of her memories. I realized that for all those years she had pretended to be stronger than she really was. Now she choked when she talked *about Caruso, she broke into a sweat when she described how he per-spired, she trembled when she tried to recall his face. Telling me what had happened between the two of them had cost her dearly. It cost her the part of her life that had stopped, in a way, a part that had remained young and then suddenly aged when she opened the doors to all her secrets and all her disappointments. The only part of her that was still healthy was joined to the sickness of her body. My mother died when she finally brought up the unbroken stone of her great love.*

And so, on this second of August, because I saw how affected she was and didn't want her upset again, instead of asking her to go on with her story I left her in the care of a neighbor and decided to use the time to visit a music critic, a man called Abadelio Trujillo.

His name and phone number had been given to me by the wife of Vicente Pérez Navarro, who went so far as to suggest that Trujillo, who still wrote for the Diario de la Marina, might have some surpris-ings facts: he had been present when Caruso reappeared in Santa Clara, and had heard his performance at the Caridad Theater.

Arranging the appointment was very simple, as was going to his house, since he lived near me, on Calle Obispo. At Abadelio Trujillo's house I was received by his brother Israel, who happened to be visiting that day. Israel was about forty-five, a quiet, meticulous man, a watchmaker who lived in the town of Güines, not in Havana. He withdrew discreetly when I sat down to talk with Abadelio, who began by saying that in 1920 he was a young reporter, too young, a boy who wanted to prove himself and make his mark by pursuing the great Caruso. His photographs indicated that he had always been delicate and feminine, and perhaps that effeminacy cre-ated a complicity between us. He listened to me attentively; I told him the same lie I had told everyone else: a professor wanted to write a book about Caruso and I was helping him with the interviews. He did the impossible, trying to remember each detail, uncover some clue, shed light on the blinding flash of the bomb. Thirty-two years had gone by, thirty-two long years, and when he looked back, back to those days in June in the year 1920, Abadelio opened a hidden wound: the one in his own heart.

"Destiny was to blame," he murmured, staring at a photograph from that time, a picture of himself standing in front of the Hotel Central in Santa Clara.

Just think: if the bomb hadn't exploded, Caruso wouldn't have disappeared, and no Havana newspaper would have been tempted to send a reporter to Santa Clara to interview him and find out if he had gotten away unharmed. But the bomb did explode, and it was a miracle there were no fatalities. Or perhaps there were: in the long run, everyone came out carrying his own corpse on his back.

But you came to hear about Caruso, the real Caruso, who arrived on these shores and was very different from the man people imagined. By that time he was already very ill; you couldn't tell by looking at him, but the proof is that he died a short while later. I wasn't in the theater the day the bomb exploded, though I went straight to the Hotel Sevilla and spent two nights drinking endless cups of coffee to stay awake, waiting for him to come in or go out. Some said he was locked in his room, and others swore he was hiding in Regla, in the house of a babalawo. I went to Regla, I risked my life for that story, I went all over the village, I stopped people on the streets, and most of them couldn't even tell me who the great Caruso was. You can imagine what Regla was like back then, there was a good deal of respect and loyalty for the babalawos. Not a leaf moved in that village without the head of the Lucumí brotherhood knowing about it, a black man like a tree trunk, who was named José de Calazán Bangoché—I think they called him Cheché.

I went back to Havana, and people were saying that Caruso was in Matanzas. Matanzas! What could Caruso be doing there!

Great artists can become a little eccentric, but Matanzas is a province with lots of out-of-the-way places, and where was I supposed to find him? A few days later there was a call to the paper: Bruno Zirato, Caruso's secretary, and Rafael de Armas, an impresario nicknamed "Armitas," stated that the performance at the Teatro Caridad would not be canceled, and Caruso would sing Marta. I ran to the station and caught the first train to Santa Clara. The Diario de la Marina heard other rumors, too: Caruso had suffered a nervous breakdown, made worse by the fact that his chauffeur of many years, a man named Fitzgerald, along with the butler at his house in East Hampton, had been arrested for robbery. Caruso never had luck with his drivers. Just look what happened with his first wife, Ada Giachetti: she ran off with the family chauffeur. Caruso came home from one of his tours, and the gardener had to give him the news. They say the way he sang "Vesti la giubba" changed after that. At some point he must have thought he should have learned how to drive, but he never did, and do you know why? He was afraid to because of an accident Puccini had. Caruso was very affected at seeing him so bruised and battered: Puccini had inhaled some fumes and broken a few bones. From that moment on Caruso refused to drive, he didn't even want to learn how to start a car.

I learned all this, and many other things, on the trip that changed my life. I had just turned twenty-one, my birthday was in May; I was a baby, an innocent kid. When I got to Santa Clara I went to the local offices of the newspaper, where the managing editor, a Spaniard named Cipriano Rivas, and his secretary, a mulatto who was also his driver, were waiting for me. Another man happened to be there, very elegant in his linen suit and white spats and a broad-brimmed hat that he wore tilted forward. I sneaked a look at what was under the hat and discovered a hard, heavily lined face, a weather-beaten face with narrow blue eyes. He was an older man, not very tall but quite robust, who stood with his legs far apart, those strong, straight legs.

The editor welcomed me, introduced me to his secretary, the mulatto was named Everado and he gave me a rather contemptuous look. Then he introduced me to the man in the hat, who seemed to me like a peasant burned by the sun, a peasant trapped inside those fine clothes. His name was Belarmino Villa; he had a tobacco business and was a great fan of the opera. He had come to the office, in fact, to make sure Caruso was going to sing that night. Then we all decided to go the theater to see if they were setting up the scenery, and maybe talk to the impresario, this man "Armitas," who people said was a very tough customer. On the way we passed a café, and since it started to rain pretty hard, we went in for something to drink. The place was crowded with people, and Cipriano Rivas nudged me with his elbow and said: "See that good-looking mulatta? . . . That's Caruso's girlfriend, she came here with him." I looked at the good-looking mulatta, and she wasn't exactly good-looking, she was voluptuous, a mix of mulatta and Chinese, but with delicate features—you could see the Cantonese touch there and in her eyes. This Cipriano Rivas was a vulgar man, he tried to hide it, but basically he was vulgar. He went up to that woman and had the gall to ask her about Caruso. Her response was very discreet: she got up and went out into the storm.

While Cipriano was circling around this woman, I started a conversation with Belarmino Villa. Beneath his rough appearance was an exquisitely refined man who knew hundreds of stories about the opera and who admired Enrico Caruso above all else. All else, in those days, could be reduced to a single name: Hipólito Lázaro. Cubans who followed the opera were divided into two camps. The Lázaro camp was more active—after all, Lázaro was married to a Cuban—but Belarmino belonged to the other camp, and he invited me to his house to fill me in on all the details.

They wouldn't let us into the theater; they said that Caruso was rehearsing and couldn't see us just then but would receive us later that afternoon, half an hour before the performance. Then I went to the hotel, the only decent hotel in Santa Clara back in those days, it's the one you see in the photograph, and I bathed and changed my clothes. Shortly after twelve I hired a Ford and gave the driver Belarmino Villa's address, he lived on the outskirts of the city, in the district called Ancora, in an elegant mansion with gardens and a butler wearing a frock coat. This butler, a cold man who didn't look Cuban, led me to the living room, where Belarmino was waiting for me. I supposed he must have bathed too, because his hair was damp and some drops of water were running down his face, and I could smell his cologne, 4711. I never forgot it because I also fell in love with that scent.

We talked about the opera, about Caruso, about Esperanza Iris. He showed me albums, souvenirs of his trips to New York and Europe. He had kept everything: programs, posters, tickets for his box—he always reserved a box. An extremely old servant, an emaciated black woman who wore the sort of petticoats they used in the last century, came into the room to serve us a kind of punch. Belarmino opened the doors of his bar—it was a revolving bar—and he took out a bottle of cognac, poured a splash into my glass, and another into his. While he was pouring he asked if I was married, and I told him I was still living with my family: my father, who was a customs inspector in Havana, and my mother, who had set up a typing school in our house. My older sister was a teacher, and my brother Israel had been studying to be an engineer but left school to go into the jewelry business.

Belarmino brought out a box of photographs: Farrar, Patti, Jeritza. There was a picture with a dedication from the famous Tita Ruffo, and another from Jean de Reszke, de Reszke along with his brother, both of them dressed as clowns, he said it was a unique pho-

tograph, the most valuable one he owned. Suddenly, among the photographs, was one of a naked boy. Belarmino turned pale, stared at it for a moment, then looked at me to see if I had seen it too. The boy was blond and had raised his eyes to look up at an indefinite spot on the ceiling, but more than a boy he seemed like a bird to me, he had the body of a white bird stretched out on a rumpled divan. Belarmino said, "Forgive me, I don't know what that photo's doing here," and he moved it away and laid it face down on a table. He looked at me again and must have seen my astonished face, twenty-one is twenty-one, after all. "Forgive me," he said, in a different, much warmer voice, and lowered his eyes. I felt I ought to say something but I didn't know what. He mumbled some words I didn't hear, he said them without looking at me, and he put his hand on my knee. It was a huge, heavy, freckled hand, the peasant hand of a man who wasn't exactly in tobacco but in cattle. My hand, by contrast, was such a small thing, so thin, so delicate, the hand of a reporter who was just starting out, a soft little fish, that's what it looked like to me, that's what it must have looked like to him when he laid my hand on his. "Think nothing of it," I said, my voice breaking, I didn't know how to tell certain lies.

Later on, he told me what he had found out about Caruso: that he was the guest of the Berenguer family but had brought a woman with him, not his wife, of course, but someone he'd met in Havana. Nobody knew who she was or where he had found her, but Zirato had rented a little house on Callejón de Plácido, very close to the theater, and the woman was staying there. Belarmino wasn't sure if this woman was the one Cipriano Rivas had approached in the café. The great Caruso, after all, was very fond of adventures. A few years back, in the zoo in New York, he had been arrested for pinching a woman's bottom. I said that great singers tend to be eccentric, and Caruso was no exception, but I'm certain that when he came to Cuba he was going through a very bad period.

That day, before the performance, I interviewed him. Belarmino Villa came with me to the interview, which was very brief. Caruso refused to talk about the robbery of his wife, Dorothy, for which they were holding his chauffeur. He also refused to talk about the bomb, claiming that the police were still investigating and he couldn't give out any details. All he wanted to talk to me about was his next season at the Metropolitan and the arias he planned to record in September. I noticed the dark circles under his eyes, and his uneasiness, as if he was expecting to hear bad news at any moment.

Hanging over him was the problem of the anonymous letters. He had received many threats. In my opinion, Caruso was frightened; you could see it in the way he moved, less in the way he sang: that immense voice still came booming out of his throat. That night there was a terrible storm in Santa Clara. The hall lit up with every flash of lightning, and Caruso's voice could be heard clearly outside the theater, for several blocks around. The people who couldn't pay for tickets sat in the park and listened to the singer as if they were inside; they said his voice made the trees tremble and his high notes woke the birds. And then there was a tremendous crash of thunder; we could hear it in the theater, almost directly over our heads. Caruso was singing with Besanzoni and he looked up at the ceiling: "Is it another bomb?" He said it in Italian and people took it as a joke, easily slipped into a not very dramatic scene of Marta.

The next day we left for Cienfuegos. It wasn't part of my original plan, but I wired the Diario de la Marina and told them I would follow the tenor and write an article about his final performance in Cuba. Belarmino had already made reservations at the Teatro Terry, which is where Caruso would sing, and we rode in the same train he was traveling on and were lucky enough to be in the car next to his. A luxurious car, outfitted expressly for the great singer, it had a sign forbidding entry to reporters and other curiosity seekers.

What I'm going to tell you now only Belarmino and I saw. I never wrote anything about it, I never discussed it with anyone. Belarmino was in the Caruso camp, he said there were things an honorable reporter should not print, he said it and put his hand on my shoulder. We were traveling at night; in those days the trains were slow. Since we weren't sleepy—understand, we were going through a delicate moment too, joyous but delicate—Belarmino and I left our compartment to talk. We were standing by a window and he was telling me stories about the opera, which I soon realized was a world of rivalry and deceit, a world filled with envy. I don't know if it's still the same. Then we saw a kind of apparition coming along the corridor. Belarmino saw it first and took his watch out of his pocket and realized it was after three in the morning. He thought it was one of the machinists or a guard; he signaled to me to take a look, and I knew right away that the person coming toward us was Enrico Caruso. He was wrapped in a bedspread, a fringed cover that looked like a tablecloth. He didn't see us; in his condition he couldn't see us. Belarmino and I discovered at the same time that he was barefoot, sweating a great deal, and gasping as if he had just run a race. But the worst thing was his eyes, those clouded eyes that had been dimmed in just a matter of hours.

Belarmino knew how to speak to a great singer. He ran to him and said something like: "Commendatore, is anything wrong?" Caruso didn't answer, he leaned against the wall; and his head bounced back and forth with the movement of the train. We thought he was on the verge of collapse, and the two of us helped him into our compartment and sat him down, and then we realized the man was naked, we could see his enormous white belly under the bedspread. "Commendatore," said Belarmino, "wouldn't you like a glass of water?" His eyes were like slits. I had a horrible feeling, I was certain he was going to die right there, right then, in our compartment. And suddenly out came a deep, solemn voice, a voice that was like a knife: "Che dissi? No! . . . Non è ver! . . . Sogno!"

Belarmino, who spoke Italian, translated for me. I asked him if he didn't think Caruso was drunk, and he assured me the Commendatore drank very little. At that moment the woman appeared, the same woman we had seen at the café in Santa Clara, not a good-looking mulatta but a sensual female with her hair hanging loose, a stunning creature who could have suckled an entire regiment. "Is he with you?" was all she said, and we didn't have time to respond because without waiting for our answer she came into the compartment. She passed her hand over Caruso's face, she held his head; it was rolling back and forth, without will, without strength. He vomited, he pissed himself and vomited at the same time, and I felt a wave of nausea, a bad attack of vertigo. Belarmino had to hold me in his arms, and I've always thought that what saved me was the smell of his cologne, the scent of 4711.

The woman had a handkerchief and wiped the vomit off Caruso's chin. Then she turned to us: I must have looked weak to her, I was so pale and dizzy, and she chose Belarmino and asked him to help her take Caruso back to his compartment. Between the two of them they did, Caruso was gradually coming to, and when Belarmino asked him if he could walk, he nodded. The three of them moved along the corridor: first the woman, opening the doors, and Caruso and Belarmino behind her. Belarmino supported him under his arms.

Although I hurried along beside them and could look into the little room that had been arranged as a bedroom for the singer, I couldn't hear what they said. The woman talked to Belarmino very quietly, looking into his eyes. I had the impression she was asking him for something. Then I heard Caruso's voice; he spoke in Italian, and I could hear his words but couldn't understand them. A few minutes later, when we were alone again, Belarmino told me that Caruso had suffered a nightmare: he had associated the movement of the train with the earthquake in San Francisco, in his sleep he had relived the terror he had felt years earlier, and when he woke in the darkness he had thrown on a blanket and started to run. Finding himself in our compartment, with two men he didn't recognize—at that late hour and in those circumstances it was impossible for him to recall our interview—had been a terrible shock for him. Belarmino supposed that Caruso thought he had finally been kidnapped, which explained his reaction: it was fear that made him vomit.

Deep down I felt that Belarmino was hiding something from me. I wanted to know what the woman had whispered to him, and I especially wanted to know the meaning of what Caruso had said when he found himself back in his own compartment. Belarmino refused to tell me, instead he put his hand under my chin and obliged me to look at him; I was totally changed, my life at last had direction, I had no need to prove myself or make my mark writing a stupid article. I had proven myself by feeling this . . . this definitive emotion, this perfect pain: you understand what I'm saying.

In Cienfuegos everything went into a spin: my life and Belarmino's, Caruso's, and that woman's; one of the musicians even died suddenly in the middle of a rehearsal. As if we all had to end up there to have the truth shaken out of us, good or bad. In my case it was good, but only for a little while, because Belarmino died a year later. In the case of Caruso, I think it was bad. His life filled with shadows: it darkened in the most incomprehensible way. I don't know everything but I do know they tried to run away, he and the woman, like a pair of lunatics. In Havana he ran away dressed as Radamés, he was seen on Calle Consulado, and all the newspapers published the story. Well, he ran out of the Teatro Terry dressed as Rodolpho, wearing that scarf and an overcoat in the middle of June. She went on the boat with him, they ran away to Castillo de Jagua and from there to Trinidad, where they suffered their misfortune.

I suggest you find this man: Benito Terry, a physician, and a descendant of the Tomás Terry for whom they named the theater.

He treated both of them, Caruso and the woman who went with him; she seemed so strong to me, but she crumbled at the end. The truth is that all of us, sooner or later, are doomed to the same fate: we become the dust of our happiness, the cloud that hovers over the explosion of our soul. I'm still a journalist and, thanks to Belarmino, an honorable one. There wasn't one bomb, there were many. All the ones that changed us that summer, all the ones that blew us to bits.

Fuggire! . . .

All night we listened to the rain. It let up for a little while at dawn and then stopped again when Enrico left to go to a lunch in his honor at the Berenguers' house, the same house where he'd been the night before. I used the time to wash my hair, I sat at the window to comb it out and stayed there for a while, looking at the houses on Callejón de Plácido, houses of ordinary people who came to their windows, too, to watch the rain falling and the water running down into the sewers. A bird floated past on the current, then its dark body got caught on the stones and stayed there, rolling back and forth, as sad as a handkerchief.

During this time when I was alone I thought about my family. About my mother, but also about my godfather, José de Calazán. I had a certain doubt about Calazán—more than a doubt, a suspicion: it was hard for me to believe it had all been so easy, that he hadn't made it harder for me to follow Enrico. I thought about Noro Cheng, my dead father, and about the father I had who was alive: a father who was like a dream. I didn't want to think about my dead, I didn't want to think about them on a day so full of bad omens. I left the window and fixed a little lunch with whatever was in the house. I ate by myself, counting the flowers on the tablecloth, shaking my head to make my hair dry faster. This hair of mine always took a long time to dry: it was Chinese hair but very thick.

Then I lay down on the bed and I stared up at the ceiling, the way I had seen Enrico do, and it occurred to me he might not come back, that he'd leave me in that house, on that rainy day, lying there for who knows how long. And so I got drowsy and then I fell asleep, a restless sleep because my damp hair bothered me, and then I woke with a start, confused by the sound of voices. I walked out of the bedroom and saw Enrico in the middle of the living room, moving his arms around in a strange way and shouting at Zirato, who was busy writing something and didn't look up. At that moment Punzo and Mario came in, dragging a trunk, and Fucito started to fold some sheets of music. Enrico stopped talking, he slammed his hand down on the table, then he turned and saw me there, watching him, not saying anything, waiting for him to finish being angry. He took a deep breath and came to me. He stroked my hair—it was still damp—then he asked why I'd ever decided to wash my hair on such a rainy day. I didn't answer; I didn't tell him the truth because he would have taken the truth as a reproach: I had washed it out of boredom, out of loneliness, and because I was a little angry.

He asked me to help him undress, he said the liquor he drank at the Berenguers' had made him dizzy. I took off his tie and unbuttoned his shirt, I made him sit on the edge of the bed so I could take off his shoes. I caressed his feet through his socks, I squeezed his toes one by one. Yuan Pei Fu had told me: the caress that begins there is the caress that goes straight to the soul. Enrico complained about having to sing in Cienfuegos; he didn't want to go there but didn't feel like going back to Havana either, much less New York. He was breathing very fast and it was hard for me to understand his words, they came to me in bits and pieces: he was talking about a lot of things at once, one complaint ran into another, until he whispered in a very husky voice that all he thought about was Naples, the sea at Naples, and the only thing he cared about was going back there. And then he got into bed, asked me to lie down with him, and fell asleep.

The train to Cienfuegos was delayed because of the rain. Two men came to tell us that sections of track were flooded and it would be better for us to wait in the house instead of at the station. Enrico passed the time drawing me, dozens of drawings that showed me naked, from the front and from the side; drawings of my face smiling and of my face not smiling, a face that looked too serious to be mine. When he got tired of drawing me he started in on Fucito; he drew him naked, conducting an orchestra of monkeys. When he was finished, I asked him to think about the Berenguers and draw them for me so I could see what they looked like, even if it was just on paper. After a while he handed me a drawing of a bald man with his mouth open, and a woman in a pearl necklace. Finally, about midnight, they told us the train was ready to leave. The trunks were at the station with Punzo, and we got into a carriage pulled by horses: it would have been impossible to get a car through those muddy streets.

At the station we found a group of men and women who had come to say goodbye. They applauded when they saw Enrico get out of the carriage. Some looked at me out of the corner of their eyes, they must have thought I was his maid, or the wife of one of his servants. Zirato had reserved several compartments, the biggest one for Enrico and me; he had made a kind of bed out of pillows and linen sheets that he'd bought in Santa Clara. As soon as the train started to move, Enrico took off his clothes and wrapped himself in the spread. He said he'd be more comfortable that way, though I thought he wasn't going to be comfortable no matter what he did. Mario, his valet, came in often to ask how we were, and Punzo kept bringing us cool drinks and clean towels. The towels were for drying off Enrico, who was sweating again as though everything inside him had turned to water and that water couldn't wait to leave his body.

Since he'd slept in the afternoon, he said he felt wide awake. But I was so tired I couldn't stand up, and my eyes started to close and the movement of the train put me in a kind of stupor, so that his conversation sounded very far away. He felt like talking that night. He talked about the time when he had only one shirt, and his father's wife washed it in the morning so it would be clean for him at night. He remembered the day he had to have his picture taken wrapped in a bedspread ("just like I am now," he said), the first photograph of him as an artist, the first one taken for a newspaper, because when the photographer came to the house his shirt was still wet. He remembered his friends from Naples; and the day he learned about his father's death: he was on a ship and they handed him a note; and the day he was told his sister Assunta had died, his little Assunta, dead of consumption while he was singing in Buenos Aires. And finally he talked about a train trip he had taken in Russia, and when he talked about that trip he remembered Ada Giachetti and how they sang together in Russia. I turned my face away and tried to concentrate on the noise the train was making. I didn't want to hear about that woman; something in her, or in the story of her and Enrico, made me furious. "She didn't even care about the children," he wailed in that tone of voice, with that grief from long ago. "I begged her not to go, but still she left us." I covered my face and squeezed my eyelids shut; I squeezed so hard my eyes began to hurt. I don't know if Enrico knew, I don't know if he realized how I hated that woman. A hate that didn't seem to make sense because Ada was an old woman by now and lived far away, in Argentina I think, and Enrico had another wife, an American my age. After this he stopped talking, and I slept for a while. And had strange dreams: I dreamed about the crippled Chinaman in the house on Calle Manrique, the one who cut out little paper dolls; and about my mother and Conga Mariate, both of them asking me to go back to Regla. But I also dreamed about Ada: Ada herself appeared in my dream, a gray-haired, spiteful woman just like Ester, Baldomero's wife, she had the same eyes, those eyes that caused fever and tears, those eyes that made you want to spit and bury them, cover them with earth so they couldn't hurt anybody else.

I woke at the sound of a thud, a noise I heard in my sleep, or maybe it was a sudden movement. I discovered that Enrico wasn't in the compartment but his clothes were, all his clothes were there. I jumped up; I was afraid he'd gone out naked. I looked in the corridor and in Mario's and Punzo's compartments, I could see through the glass that they were both asleep, and I started walking. I didn't open my mouth; I was thinking the most awful things: that he'd thrown himself off the train or that somebody had kidnapped him. I walked to the next car; it was only the second time I'd been on a train and it was hard for me to keep my balance. And then I saw two men: one of them was going in and out of a compartment, and the other stayed in the corridor, terrified, looking inside. I ran toward them. I could tell from their faces that Enrico had to be close by. And they realized I was looking for him and stepped aside for me. Then I saw him, but it was like seeing another man: his arms hung limp, the spread covered his shoulders but not his chest and belly. He looked like a lost child, or one of those poor old men who have no place to go, but most of all he looked like a maniac. I called his name a few times, he squinted his eyes and almost closed them, sleepy-looking eyes that were falling into a kind of pit. I went over to him and lifted his head, and suddenly he vomited at my feet; his skin was cold but almost dry: the only time in all the time we were together that his skin wasn't covered in sweat.

At first I didn't know who the men were, I thought they were a father with his son. The one who looked like the father offered to help me—he said his name but I was so nervous I hardly heard him, and between the two of us we dragged Enrico back, and not long after that he came to and took a few sips of cool water and looked at me; he didn't ask any questions, he just knew who I was. He said he'd had a bad dream, and from the way he talked I had the feeling his bad dream wasn't over yet, part of him was still lost in the nightmare. The man who had helped me with Enrico realized he ought to leave us alone, and he said goodbye, calling him *Commendatore*. He said it with respect; he didn't care about the state Enrico was in, soiled with his own vomit, stinking of sweat, soaked in piss. I stopped the man before he left, I begged him not to tell anybody what he'd seen, and to please tell his son not to say anything either. The man shook his head and looked at me with his narrow eyes; he had a strong face like a peasant, a broad face with blue eyes.

"Nobody admires the great Caruso more than I," he said. "As for my son, the person you see there is an honorable man."

He turned away, and I never saw him again.

I woke up Mario and Punzo. Enrico still wasn't himself. He mentioned his nightmare again, a nightmare about an earthquake. Mario told me that Enrico really had lived through an earthquake, but that was years ago and he couldn't understand why it had come back to haunt him now. Fucito got up, too, and came to the compartment with his own favorite remedy: a cup of milk mixed with cognac. Enrico drank it down and lit a cigarette; it seemed to me he was finally waking up. Punzo, who often talked about sickness, blamed the attack on the lunch he'd eaten at the Berenguers' house. Fucito only said that vomiting had saved him.

I began to clean Enrico as though he were still the way he was in the other compartment—still a little boy or an old man with no place to go. I rubbed him down with cologne, I fanned him before I gave him clean clothes, I combed his hair while he smoked, and while I was doing that he took my hand.

"Listen to me carefully, Aïda." I was afraid, I thought he was having another nightmare. I tried to look into his eyes to see if he was all there, if he was in his right mind, or if he had fallen back into his bad dream. "Listen to me: I didn't have any nightmare, and it wasn't indigestion. Somebody tried to poison me." I kneeled in front of him, I put my hands on his thighs, I asked him how he knew.

"I know they gave me something." His mind was clear, and I thought his eyes looked sincere—those eyes were looking straight at me. "They're going to kill me in Cienfuegos, now I'm sure, and I don't have much time left."

The compartment was very big, it was really two compartments joined together, but it seemed too small because of all the pillows and our makeshift bed. I felt caged in—it was an awful feeling, a panic that the noise of the train made worse.

"Save yourself," Enrico said. "I don't want them to kill you too."

I didn't answer but I leaned against his body, I put my ear to his cold belly. It smelled of cologne: I was sure his belly was giving me a message.

"We'll run away," I said.

Enrico shook his head, he tried to smile, but he was really terrified.

"Where can we run to, Aïda?"

I was twenty-seven years old, but life had taken everything from me: husband, daughter, it had even taken my father, or given me one father instead of the other. It couldn't take anything else. I got out Enrico's clothes, I helped him to button his shirt, I put on his shoes and socks, I looked at him with fire in my eyes—now I was the one who looked like a maniac, like a wild animal ready to grab him by the neck and drag him away. I told him that when we got to Cienfuegos I'd find out where we could go, but he couldn't tell anybody, not Zirato or Mario, least of all Punzo. I didn't like Punzo. All he had to do was get some money and trust me. José de Calazán had friends in the brotherhoods in other towns, he knew the *babalawos* in other provinces, I'd heard him talk lots of times about his *ecobios* in Trinidad. If I needed to, I'd call on my godfather's name. I was sure we'd find help.

He kept saying he couldn't run away, he couldn't stay in a foreign country, certainly not in Cuba, what would happen to him there? For the first time, I raised my voice to him, I let my rage out. I felt rage, and fear too, and a passion to defend him and defend myself. I'm not sure if I was defending you too, Enriqueta. Now that I'm telling you about it, it's clearer to me: I think somehow my body knew you were inside, struggling for the same thing, to keep him with us and get him away from all that misfortune.

"Would it be better if they killed you?" I didn't even recognize my own voice. "Would it be better if they set off another bomb, or poisoned you the way they did today?"

Enrico puffed on his cigarette and leaned his head back.

"They won't let me go with you," I shouted. I was crying. "Even if they don't kill you, I'd have to say goodbye to you."

Then he lowered his eyes, it seemed to me he was thinking it over, and I kept quiet. One of the few things I've learned in my life is that you have to let men think. Without opening his eyes, he whispered what only he knew:

"There are too many people who'll be better off if I'm dead."

"That's exactly why," I said. "Let's run away in Cienfuegos— we can leave from the theater."

I was so desperate I came up with the idea. It may seem crazy now, back then it was even crazier: we'd never been in Cienfuegos, we didn't know where the theater was or what we'd have to do to run away. But at that moment it was all decided and sealed with my kiss. Enrico called me to him and I put my arms around him and swore I'd never leave him.

When we got to Cienfuegos a crowd of admirers was waiting for him. Enrico looked wonderful, clean and perfumed in his white suit and two-tone shoes. Nobody could ever have guessed how terrified he'd been the night before. I don't know if Zirato suspected anything about our plans, but I think Mario did. He took my hand while we were watching Enrico sign autographs, he squeezed my hand and said he knew his boss was fond of me. I stared into his eyes, I knew right away he was trying to tell me something.

"Don't let him do anything crazy. You know he has to sing in Mexico."

I must have had an angry Yemayá that morning, a fierce Yemayá inside my body, an eye of water that saw everything and crushed it.

"I don't rule him, Mario," I said, and pulled my hand away. "I don't rule over him, but I will take care of him. Don't you worry."

I wanted to interview Dr. Benito Terry, but to do that I would have had to travel to Cienfuegos, and for the moment that was impossible. My mother could no longer take care of herself, and I had to hire a woman, a neighbor of ours on Calle Amargura, to look after her during the day. In the evening, when I came home from work, I bathed and fed her, and then I would help her to a rocking chair, and sit with her, and we would talk until I saw that she was too tired, or too sad. Sometimes she was the one who decided to stop.

I wanted to earn some extra money, and so in addition to my parts in soap operas, I began to write commercials for the Blue Network. I was also asked to report the news, and so, with one thing and another, I didn't stop talking all day. Fortunately I never lost my voice, perhaps because from the very beginning I always took care of my throat with the home remedies recommended by other announcers. At night I would gargle, and I often took a spoonful of honey mixed with a drop of iodine. This was how I cleaned my instrument, as Caruso would have said. In fact, if I inherited anything from him, it was his throat. My mother had told me that Caruso's throat was a liquid cave, and that mine was exactly like his. You could hear it in my voice: it was round and clean and had a kind of natural resonance.

Since I couldn't interview Dr. Terry, I decided to find a person my mother still remembered with affection. Thirty-two years after my parents met in the kitchen of the Hotel Inglaterra, the cook who witnessed it, Violeta Anido, was living in her hometown of Consolación del Sur, where she had opened a little food stand that was run now by her children. A sister of Violeta's, with whom my mother had always stayed in touch, gave me her address; the town was just a couple of hours from Havana.

One day I decided to go to see her, and I got up at dawn and caught a train to Consolación. Violeta didn't have a phone, but her sister had said she almost never left town. In the morning she went to the stand, a habit she hadn't broken; she would look everything over and help prepare lunch. By this time she was an elderly woman of seventy-four, which meant she was forty-two years old when the bomb exploded.

As soon as I reached Consolación I looked for her house, and found it locked. A neighbor told me that Violeta was at her place, which was very close by, and I could walk there if I wanted, or wait for her on the porch, because she usually got back before noon. I decided to wait, and I sat on a chair and asked myself if a trip that was so unplanned would turn out to be worthwhile. After a short time I saw an extremely fat woman coming down the street. I didn't remember her at all, but from the way she started to hurry and kept looking at the house, I knew it was Violeta. I walked toward her and said good morning, and she put on an extremely serious face. I smiled and tried to sound very respectful: "I've come from Havana. I'm Enriqueta, Aida Cheng's daughter."

She was startled, or perhaps she simply hesitated for a few seconds. I saw that her dress was stained, and her whole body gave off a dense odor, like stewed vegetables. She put a hand to her head, then she came close and took me by the arm. "Enriqueta, baby, if I passed you on the street I wouldn't know you."

The last time Violeta Anido had seen me I was seven or eight years old, but she said that if she looked closely, she would have recognized the little dimple on my chin, and my eyes, they were a mix of other eyes she knew so well.

"And you have your mother's hair," she went on. "What's new with poor Aidita?"

I didn't tell her much, I didn't say her disease was terminal; it didn't seem a good idea at the time. Violeta invited me to have lunch, and we talked about my work and my life. She said it was a shame I hadn't married. In those days, turning thirty without a husband meant you'd never have one. Neither of us knew I would, within the year, and that he would be the watchmaker Israel Trujillo, the brother of Abadelio, the music critic I had interviewed a few days earlier.

"I've come to see if you remember anything," I admitted to Violeta. "My mother is telling me everything, but sometimes she forgets dates or people's names. She was the one who suggested I come."

Violeta sighed and began to clean her teeth with a toothpick.

"I remember everything. What do you want me to tell you?"

"Whatever you can," I said. "What you saw that afternoon in the kitchen, how they met, how they looked."

She broke the toothpick in two and held the pieces in her hand.

"I saw them that afternoon, I was there when they left together, I thought they'd gone forever. When Aidita came back she was in very bad shape. I don't know how she survived: it's a miracle you're both alive, because you were already on the way, you went through it all."

We returned to the porch and sat down, and I took out my notebook.

"What are you writing for?"

"It's my parents' story," I told her. "I want to know what happened between them. If I don't write it down, I won't be able to remember it later."

Violeta looked out at some tamarind trees that were making a strange sound in the wind and shook her head slowly. She had warts on her neck, and her movements and huge size made her seem like an old animal, a serene and powerful animal.

I've never told anybody. I promised your grandmother, poor Domitila Cuervo, may she rest in peace. Reporters came to see me, they offered me money, all those people came to the kitchen at the Inglaterra and they all wanted to know the same thing: if it was true that Enrico Caruso had been there. At the time I swore to God I wouldn't open my mouth, and I threatened the boys who worked with me in the kitchen—they were good boys, but I had to threaten them. The only way to make them keep quiet was to tell them that your grandfather, Yuan Pei Fu, had an opium den and a gang of Chinamen who would cut any big-mouth to pieces. And it wasn't a lie, Enriqueta. But then there was your godfather: everybody in

Havana knew him, at least they'd heard about the babalawo José de Calazán Bangoché. In that way your mother was lucky. Nobody wanted those two for enemies: not Cheché—that was what they called Calazán—and not the paisano on Calle Manrique. Yuan Pei Fu had other businesses too: all that paisano gambling—Chi Fa, Mah-jongg, Ku Pai—those were all his. He was a powerful Chinaman; he gave his orders and didn't have to move a finger.

What happened that day was that your mother came to give me some sewing, some blouses Domitila made for me. Your grandmother didn't have to sew for a living: Yuan Pei Fu gave her everything she needed. He was the one who bought your house on Calle Amargura, and he was the one, back at the beginning, who gave Noro Cheng, your grandfather on paper, the money to open the laundry.

Your mother came to the kitchen and she looked uneasy; she gave me the blouses and sat down on a stool where I used to sit when I prepared meat. She was nervous, she took her time on purpose, she made conversation with me so she could stay for a while. Then I offered her lemonade—I always made some because it was so hot in the kitchen—and just when I was handing it to her we heard that boom, that huge explosion. The boys who helped me in the kitchen ran out to the street and shouted that a bomb had gone off in the theater. Aidita wanted to go outside too. She had loosened her hair and she looked very pale, I had to hold on to her to keep her inside. Five or six minutes went by, maybe a little more. She told me to let go of her, she had to go out, if she stayed there she would die of sorrow. And that's when Caruso appeared.

I didn't recognize him. He wore a costume, but he was dirty, covered with dust from the bomb, even his face was black with soot. Aidita ran over to him and they hugged, they talked very low, she grabbed a cloth I was holding and wet it and began to clean his face. Meanwhile I filled another glass with lemonade and offered it to

Caruso. I still didn't know it was him, I didn't know what to think, I was so confused by the explosion and by the things your mother was doing.

He looked up when I gave him the glass. I saw his face—it was clean now—and then I recognized him. I remember I shouted "Holy God," and I put my hand on your mother but she didn't even react, she was so taken by that man. After a while Caruso asked if he could stay there, in the Hotel Inglaterra, because he didn't want to go back to his hotel, it was the Hotel Sevilla. Aidita was like a tiger; she said she'd take him to a safe place. I tried to stop her, I asked her if she knew what she was doing, if she knew who that man was. She said she did, and that José de Calazán was waiting for them. "This is Cheché's business," she told me, and she meant I should stay out of it.

One of the boys who worked in the kitchen came in and started to laugh when he saw Caruso in his costume. Aidita asked me to send him out for a taxi, and I did. I thought about Domitila and wondered if she agreed with what her daughter was doing. Your mother was a widow, she'd had a little girl who died too, I couldn't imagine her mixed up in this kind of adventure with an older man, a man who was so famous; she couldn't hope for anything good to come of it. The taxi came and Aidita gave me a kiss. I was fond of her and sorry for her because of what she had suffered. She looked very happy to me, she left with Caruso, they disappeared into the night.

Two days later I went to see your grandmother. I went out of curiosity, I don't deny it, but I also went because it was my obligation. Aidita had left my kitchen with that man, that's why I felt responsible for her. When I got to your house on Calle Amargura it was locked, but your grandmother Domitila was inside. She was frantic, she said your mother had gone crazy, she didn't know what she was doing, and Cheché and Yuan Pei Fu couldn't do anything with her.

She confided in me. She told me it had started in May. She didn't know where Aidita and Caruso had met, but she thought it was somewhere near the Hotel Sevilla. Somebody told her that Caruso saw her crossing the street and told the driver to stop the car he was riding in so he could see her up close. They talked, and Caruso fell head over heels in love. I'm going to tell you something, Enriqueta, so you can understand: your mother was a real beauty when she was young. That's why her first husband, Baldomero, lost his head and left his wife. After a while, when she became a widow and then had all the grief of losing her daughter, she wasn't just a beauty any-more, she became a fabulous-looking woman, she had that serious-ness, like she was onstage. She didn't even have to fix herself up, she was very tall and stood out wherever she went. And she was mixed: nothing excites men more than that mix: Chinese eyes and hair and that great mulatta body—it stopped them in their tracks. No wonder Caruso took one look and fell in love.

That day your grandmother made me promise I wouldn't tell anybody what happened at the Inglaterra. I told her she knew me well enough to know that Violeta Anido's lips were sealed. If they're open now, it's because I realize you're part of the family, the most important part of what happened, the fruit of that craziness, that bomb that stirred up all Havana.

Days went by, from time to time I'd go to Calle Amargura, I'd visit Domitila and ask if she had any news about her daughter; it made me sad to see her all alone. One night in the beginning of July, when I left work at the kitchen, I had a kind of premonition and went to her house. Your grandmother was very mysterious when she opened the door; in the living room I could see the kind of bundles you take on a trip. Sitting in a chair, looking like he was at a funeral, was José de Calazán—I never saw a meaner, darker black man. He gave me a dirty look. In the other corner, smoking, with his eyes shut tight, was Yuan Pei Fu. It scared me to death to see the two of them there together. Domitila hugged me, she was crying. "Our Aidita is dying," she said. A black woman came in from the kitchen and gave her something to drink, she said it was linden tea, and she patted her on the back. I didn't want to ask what had happened, and I waited for your grandmother to finish drinking her tea. She stopped crying and whispered to me:"We're going to her in Trinidad. She's in a very bad way, they told us to come." The black woman came back and brought tea for me; she kept going in and out of the kitchen, carrying things back and forth. Domitila took me aside and asked me to sit down: "We have to catch the train now. I don't know if I'll find her alive."

Away from Cheché's eyes, I asked her what had happened. She said nobody knew. They received a telegram telling them to come for her; it was signed by a friend of Calazán's. All they could find out was that Aidita was badly hurt and Caruso was dead.

I told her to have faith, to trust in the saints. And I stayed with her until I watched them leave: she and José de Calazán went straight to the train station; Yuan Pei Fu, who was too old for all that running around, left with some paisanos who were like his bodyguards. The black woman who had brought the tea stayed in the house on Calle Amargura, getting everything ready to take care of your mother if she came back alive.

I left with a very bad feeling. I felt as though I was part of the tragedy, that I hadn't done anything when I ought to have done something, when Caruso ran into the kitchen in a panic. But the feeling left as soon as I asked myself this question: what was it I could have done, after all? Who could have stood up to a singer as great as Enrico Caruso and a woman like Aidita? Love had made her as stubborn as a mule.

I came home, and couldn't sleep. My children were grown by then, and they asked me what was wrong, and I didn't tell the secret even to them. I had been a widow for six years, but at the *time I was in love. He was a waiter at the Hotel Quinta Avenida, he was younger than me, and we used to see each other in secret, in a room at that hotel. On the night the bomb went off, after your mother and Caruso had gone, he came by the Inglaterra and we walked over to the theater, like so many other people were doing, to see the damage from the explosion. While we were looking at the damage, he told me he was getting married in a month—he was marrying the girlfriend he'd had his whole life, I had known all about her. He said we'd go on seeing each other, but the news hurt me, it exploded in my veins and my eyes filled with tears. I hid it by looking down, and I remember it was as though the rubble on the ground was the wreckage of my own life. On the day the bomb went off, I felt old and used up for the first time. I was forty-two years old, I was a widow, and my only future was to go on being a widow. I didn't say anything to him, and we still saw each other, once or twice a week. But that night, when I came home from Domitila's house and looked at my bed, my room, my things, I knew the month of July had just started, it was July for everybody: for Caruso and your mother, a black July; for Domitila, who was on her way to Trinidad, a desperate July. And as for me—I couldn't stop thinking about his damn wedding—what would this month be like, and all the months that came after? I knew I loved that man, and I knew I had to break off with him. I stared at the ceiling and made up my mind. I cried all night: I was far away, but I kept your mother's tears company, and the tears your grandmother cried too.*

You could say the bomb was a sign, a kind of explosion that split my life in two. Months later one of the boys who helped me in the kitchen showed me a piece of tile with half a tree painted on it, he told me he'd taken it from the rubble at the theater the day after the explosion. I asked him if he would give it to me, and he said he'd be happy to, he'd picked it up just out of curiosity.

I still have that piece of tile, the half a tree that seemed like my other half: the bomb blew away a part of me. I asked my children to put it in my coffin when I die. I know that when I die, both halves will die too. If you want, I can show it to you now. . . . Come with me, Enriqueta, I'll show it to you.

Ed ella? . . .

*W*e stayed in a two-story house on Calzada de Dolores. Enrico and I were in the rooms on the second floor; they were very big and had a balcony that faced the street. Mario, Punzo, and Zirato were in the rooms downstairs, and Fucito stayed at the Hotel Gran Prado with the other artists. The only performance at the Teatro Terry was scheduled for the next day, a Saturday, and all over the city we saw posters advertising the opera.

Enrico changed his clothes. The heat was even worse after the rain, and all he wanted to wear was a white shirt and linen pants. Mario brought him a Panama hat. I liked seeing him dressed that way because he didn't look anything like a foreigner. I thought that would be a good outfit for him when we ran away.

They all decided to go to the theater, and before they left Enrico asked me if I wanted to come along. Zirato and Punzo didn't even try to hide how annoyed they were: for one thing, they didn't like me to be seen with Enrico; for another, they were afraid I was hiding something from them. You could see it in their eyes, in how much they wanted to catch some word, find out some thought of mine. I told him I would go to the theater the next day and see him when he was all dressed up and ready for the performance. I said I was planning to walk around Cienfuegos and I wanted to buy a new fan. He came close to kiss me; he kissed me on the temple and whispered:

"Do whatever you have to do."

As soon as they left I ran to the kitchen. There were two maids in the house, and I had a good feeling about one of them:

she was a black woman about my mother's age, and I liked her as soon as I saw her. I found her preparing lunch, and I sat down next to her and asked her name. She said her name was Asteria. It seemed like a very unusual name to me and I had her say it twice and then I repeated it: Asteria, Asteria. She burst out laughing, and I offered to help with the food, but she said no, she said I'd get my hands dirty. I didn't pay any attention to her, I picked up the knife and began to peel and chop just as fast as she did. Asteria looked up, she didn't say anything but we looked into each other's eyes; it was a look of understanding that said a lot of things: that we came from the same place, for example, and shared the same blood. That was when I decided to ask if she knew about any Lucumí brotherhoods in the city of Cienfuegos. She smiled, and I had an idea it puzzled her that a woman like me—I was wearing nice clothes and traveling with theater people—would ask this kind of question.

"Not in Cienfuegos. But in Palmira there's a Congo brotherhood."

Then the other maid came in; she was very young, almost a girl, and she was startled to see me sitting there. Mario had given her some of Enrico's clothes and some sheets to wash. She had come in to ask if she had to boil them, and I told her she should, and also to toss some slivers of perfumed soap into the water when she boiled them. She didn't leave, so I found some excuse to get her out of the kitchen: I sent her for some of my clothes. Asteria and I were by ourselves again, and I asked her where Palmira was.

"Four leagues from here," she said. "If you go by train you get there faster. But you can't go to Palmira and ask for the brotherhood because nobody will tell you anything. If you want them to tell you, go to Pueblo Grifo first, that's right here in Cienfuegos, and ask where Tata Sandoval's house is."

I thanked her and asked her not to say anything to anybody about Palmira. She began to slice some plantains.

"God go with you," was her answer.

I went out and saw a lot of activity on Calzada de Dolores, peddlers pushing their carts and people walking up and down. A work crew was laying what looked like trolley tracks, and I saw some cars for hire by a park. I crossed the street and asked the first driver if he could take me to Pueblo Grifo. He looked very surprised, then he asked me where in Pueblo Grifo.

"I'm going to Tata Sandoval's house," I said in a steady voice, like it was something I'd done my whole life.

The driver told me to get in, we drove down the street toward the edge of the city, and soon we were on a rough stony road with a lot of heavy brush growing along both sides. Two or three times we had to stop to let cars pass that were coming the other way. I won't deny I was afraid, leaving a strange city and going into an even stranger district. Nobody had sent me there and nobody was expecting me, I didn't even know what I was looking for. It's been thirty-two years, and I can still see myself in that car, I can see myself clearly, not going anywhere or going straight into something crazy. Now, after all these years, I finally know what I was: the horse of a power that controlled me, an animal galloping because her rider wanted her to. My rider was always Yemayá: she ruled me, she ruled over me then just like she ruled over all the moments that came later. The two of us were struggling against Orula, keeper of the Secret of Ifá, who knows the future and reveals it to men; and against Oddúa, master of the secrets of death and master of solitude; and Obba, Yewá, and Oyá, the three "death watchers" who live in cemeteries; and above all we were struggling against Osún, the messenger of Olofi, struggling against the message he brought us more than once, a message of death we did not want to hear.

We wanted to change the future Ifá had shown us, we wanted to deny the secret of Oddúa and move away the earth of cemeteries. We wanted all that, but we also held on tight to life, the thread of life that kept Enrico alive. We were two women: Yemayá and the horse she had mounted, the two of us against the will of the other *orishas*. On the way to Pueblo Grifo I put myself in the hands of God, I prayed to Father Olofi to send away his messenger—I said my prayer in a whisper and then I held my tongue—and finally I had a thought for Sanfancón, the Changó of the Chinamen.

A few minutes after we started driving along that road we saw some houses, and the car stopped in front of a general store. I asked the driver where Sandoval lived, and he answered with another question:

"Don't you know where he lives?"

I got out of the car and asked him to wait for me. I went into the store and took a deep breath and breathed in that familiar smell, the smell of food in sacks but mixed with a kind of perfume. The counter was at the front, and the storekeeper was waiting on two women, and in the back, near a window that had bars over it, was a little makeshift barbershop, where a man was cutting another man's hair. I went over to a boy who was sweeping the dirt floor, I asked him if he knew where Tata Sandoval's house was.

"That's Tata Sandoval," he answered, pointing to the man who was getting his hair cut.

When he heard his name he turned to look at me. He was a light-skinned mulatto with slicked-back hair and very manly eyes. There was a long silence, and everybody stared at me; women who were waiting near the counter moved to get a better look at me while I walked back to the barbershop.

"Tata Sandoval," I said, and my hands were sweating. "My godfather, José de Calazán Bangoché, sent me to see you."

He didn't react, and I was afraid he'd tell me he didn't know anybody by that name. He turned his head in the other direction and said something to the barber in a quiet voice, and the barber took the towel off his shoulders. Tata Sandoval stood up. He reminded me of a tailor: he had those soft movements that measure things calmly. He was much taller than me but very thin, a skeleton with a bony face, and under his guayabera he had bony shoulders. I wondered if he had consumption.

"You're Cheché's goddaughter?"

I said I was. I stood very still under a downpour of looks, and I breathed in that smell again, but now I knew it was the odor of meat mixed with the scent of shaving soap. Two more men came in and I was still the center of attention; nobody moved, none of them went back to what they were doing.

"Come to my house," said Sandoval. "My wife's there."

We left the store and walked in front of the car, and I saw that the driver had gotten out and was talking to another man. Both of them followed us with their eyes until we turned onto a narrow little street, walked around what looked an animal pen, and went into a house. Tata Sandoval offered me a rocking chair, he called to his wife and asked her to bring some juice. He didn't ask me if I wanted juice. And he didn't introduce me to his wife.

"Now tell me, what can I do for Cheché?"

The tone of his voice made me think he disliked my godfather.

"I want to know how I can find the Congo brotherhood in Palmira. I need the brotherhood's help."

Sandoval took a cigar out of his pocket.

"And what do you need their help for, if you don't mind my asking."

He lit the cigar and started to smoke. I wasn't sure if I should tell him the truth or make up some lie, a lie that would include my godfather.

"It's some business of Calazán's. I have a message for the brotherhood."

Tata Sandoval was very quick.

"If it's some business of Cheché's, why didn't he tell you how to find them?"

I had the feeling he knew I was lying, and I pretended to cough to gain a little time. Then I decided to tell him the truth.

"I need help," I said, and it was an effort for me not to burst into tears. "I'm in danger, but my godfather doesn't know about it."

"Cheché is of my blood," Sandoval said calmly. "And if it's true that you're his goddaughter, then you're my goddaughter too."

"I'm Aida Petrirena Cheng," I said. Until that moment I hadn't told him my name, and he hadn't asked me.

"A Chinese last name." Sandoval smiled. "There's a lot of Chinamen around Camajuaní, they have their own *babalawo*. They kill with paper, they do their work with crickets and dragonflies."

I said I was in Cienfuegos with another person. I lowered my voice to tell him that the person was Enrico Caruso and he was going to sing the next day in the Teatro Terry.

"They sent him a paper saying they would kill him. And me along with him, because we live together. They tried to kill him with a bomb in Havana, and my godfather had to hide him in Regla. I know they're going to try again here."

Tata Sandoval listened to the story but didn't say anything and didn't show any surprise. Suddenly he asked what the Congo brotherhood had to do with all that.

"I need them to help us get to Trinidad," I said.

Sandoval's wife came in and offered me a glass of yellow liquid that looked like sugarcane juice.

"Just for a few days," I said. "Then we'll go back to Havana and leave for Naples."

I realize now he must have thought I was crazy. Sandoval didn't know what Naples was, he didn't understand that whole story about Enrico, or the danger I was talking about, or my plan. His wife was a fat mulatta, she was dressed all in white and was wearing the beads of Ochún. In spite of what she couldn't understand, I think she understood me better than he did. She looked at her husband, she gave him the look that women know how to use when they want a man to do something.

"She's Cheché's goddaughter," he told her.

"Calazán!" the woman cried. "What a great man he is!"

Tata Sandoval told me to go back to Cienfuegos; he said he would meet me that afternoon in a shop on Calle Urrutiner, a place where they sold cloth. He would take me to the Congo brotherhood of Palmira, and we would ask Nicolás Iznaga for help. He was the authority.

I went home, and I had to eat lunch alone. Enrico had sent word that he would have lunch with his impresario and with Zirato. Asteria told me that Mario and Punzo came back at noon, but Mario felt sick and Punzo had gone out for medicine. She lowered her voice and asked me if I'd found Tata Sandoval. I said I had and asked her again not to tell anybody.

She shook her head. "God's will be done."

At three o'clock I took another car to Calle Urrutiner. I didn't write down the name of the shop where I was supposed to meet Sandoval, but I had it in my mind: La Bandera Americana. Besides cloth they sold hats and fans, and while I was waiting I asked a salesman to show me some fans. He took out half a dozen and laid them on the counter, he told me a little about each one, and then he stood there looking at me. I picked out one with sandalwood ribs, I fanned myself to smell the scent, and it was wonderful: a cool breeze with perfume. I still have the fan, I keep it with the drawings Enrico gave me. I took it to the opera on Saturday, it was with me during the adventure I had that night and all the nights that came after. I'm telling you this, Enriqueta, because I want to take it with me, I want to have it near me when the end comes, I want you to put it here, in this hand, or whatever's left of it.

Now I remember some words. When I picked out the fan, the clerk, he was a fat little man with a nose like a beak, said: "It's absolutely precious." I wasn't in the mood for jokes, but it struck me funny, it sounded so silly coming from his mouth, and I started to laugh. And while I was laughing I heard a voice, and it broke my laughter like glass:

"The train leaves in fifteen minutes."

It was Sandoval. He was wearing a hat and looked even more like a tailor, a patriotic and meticulous tailor. I paid for the fan and followed him to a car waiting for us outside. We drove to the station in that car.

"I sent word to Nicolás Iznaga," he said, not looking at me. "If we're lucky, we'll be back by six."

I used the fan for the first time on the train. It was a short ride, but very hot. In Palmira we got into a car, Sandoval talked in a low voice to the driver, who drove through the town and took all kinds of different roads until we came to what looked like a sugar plantation. There was a main house in the middle, and little houses all around it. Sandoval told the driver to wait for us, he signaled to me to follow him, and we walked to the main house. He stayed outside and called to a woman, he shouted "Felipa," and she came to the window.

"Tell Iznaga."

A few minutes went by. Sandoval lit a cigar, and I thought I would melt in the sun. A man opened the door: a black man, stout and bald, not old, not young, with a violet-colored scar that started in his eyebrows, crossed his forehead, and went around the back, as though somebody had tried to split his skull open.

"Can we come in?" Sandoval asked.

Nicolás Iznaga looked at me with distrust.

"And her? What about her?"

"She's Cheché's goddaughter. She wants to talk to you."

Felipa, the woman who had come to the window, rushed out of the house; she didn't look at us or say a word. Iznaga gestured for us to go in, and Sandoval and I followed him to a room that had an altar. He asked us to sit on the floor, on a very worn mat, as if he was going to throw the *ékuele* for us.

"Say it clear and let's not waste time," he said to me. You could see he was furious.

"I need protection. Another person and I must go to Trinidad."

He twisted his lips around. I thought he was going to spit.

"This person will pay for the services of the brotherhood," I said. "And for a place in Trinidad where we can hide, someplace out of the way."

Iznaga looked at Sandoval, I couldn't tell what kind of look it was.

"When do you want to go?" he asked me.

"Tomorrow night," I said. "It has to be tomorrow."

Tata Sandoval was sitting beside me; he bowed his head. A smell came from his slicked-back kinky hair, a smell of chamomile. Iznaga gave a weary sigh, got to his feet, and slowly walked to the altar. He stood there for a while, staring at a tureen that didn't have soup in it; it had some objects made of iron.

"I wouldn't want to get on Cheché's bad side," he murmured. "How long will you be in Trinidad?"

"Until there's no more danger. A few days, two or three weeks. Then we'll go to Naples."

Iznaga gave Sandoval that same look again, a look that left me out: I didn't know if it was a wise look or a mocking one. I think about it now and can't believe I did what I did, I can't believe I had the courage to sit there, in a brotherhood house, a house that made people afraid, between those two men who all of a sudden seemed like an invention, like two ghosts somebody had put in my way, I don't know whether it was to give me darkness or to give me light.

"The only way to do it is by sea," Iznaga said.

Then he said there was a little boat that went back and forth to Trinidad during the day. But in our case, we would have to sail at night: from the port of Cienfuegos to Castillo de Jagua, across the bay, and from there in a motorboat either to the port of Casilda or to a lonely beach called La Boca. He said La Boca would be better because not too many people would see us.

I asked him how we would get away from the theater, and he said he knew the area very well.

"Listen to what we're going to do," he whispered, making his voice sound hollow; he had a husky, changeable voice.

I listened, with all my soul I held on to his words, to the escape that was finally beginning to take shape. When I left Palmira I felt relieved; it wasn't as hot, and on the train I didn't have to use the fan. Sandoval left me in the Cienfuegos station.

"Send word if you change your mind," he grumbled.

It was late afternoon, the sun was at his back, and with the light behind him he looked even skinnier.

"Don't worry," was my answer. "I won't change my mind."

I never saw Yuan Pei Fu, my real grandfather. Not even photographs of him, because he never allowed anyone to take his picture. When I was a little girl, my grandmother Domitila took me to the house on Calle Manrique, gave the two obligatory knocks on the door, and opened it with her key, which was rusty by now. We passed through the empty living room, walked down the dark hallway, and went into a room that was like a big hardware store. Then she said: "Look, Enriqueta, this was your grandfather's bedroom."

He died a few months after I was born, and he died in the same silent, mysterious way he had lived. One of the men who lived in the house found him lying in front of the altar, his nostrils stuffed with cotton and a piece of cloth tied around his head. There were many sticks of incense burning around his body, and at first everyone believed it was a suicide. But a Chinese doctor who examined the body said my grandfather had died of natural causes, and that minutes before his death, when he knew it was the end, he had lit the incense, put on his burial clothes—a black suit that had been made to measure—and taken precautions to keep his face from becoming distorted: he had tied up his jaw and put plugs in his nose.

When he died, Yuan Pei Fu was eighty-two years old. He was the last survivor of the first group of Chinese who had come to Cuba in 1847, aboard the frigate Oquendo, and he had in his possession the first image of Sanfancón that came to these shores from China. Hundreds of paisanos attended his wake, and since the house couldn't hold so large a crowd, they had to form a line out on the street: they entered the room in groups of four, paid their respects to my grandfather's remains, offered condolences to my grandmother, and went out again, their heads bowed.

The image of Sanfancón remained in the house for a few years, in the care of another Chinese who had always been like my grandfather's shadow, a servant or an assistant who prepared his meals and announced his visitors. When he died, the image was removed and taken to an unknown location. Some said it was in the city of Matanzas, at the headquarters of a secret society called Hen Yi Tong (The Brothers). Others said the Sanfancón of Yuan Pei Fu had actually been replaced by another, identical image on the night my grandfather died, and the original moved to the town of Sagua la Grande, where it passed into the hands of a California Chinese who owned a sugar mill in the area.

While my grandmother was alive, some of Yuan Pei Fu's friends would visit her from time to time. And my grandmother continued to visit them, but not as frequently as before; I once heard her say it made her sad to go to Calle Manrique. When she died, the connection was all but broken. My mother returned only once to the house where her real father had lived, and then it was to attend another funeral: that of the cripple who had cut out little paper figures, and who, despite being a cripple, or perhaps because of it, died a very old man. I was twenty at the time. I went with my mother to the wake, and that was the last time either of us set foot in the house.

But in November 1952, when my mother was confined to her bed and both of us were approaching that point of no return, that painful place in her story, I suddenly felt a need to go back to my grandfather's house, to go in and find a memory, an air, a sob that might still be wandering among the walls stained by the smoke of incense and, perhaps, the smoke of opium.

One morning I woke up with the idea in mind. I went to the Blue Network as always, left shortly before noon, and, since I didn't have to be back until three, I used the time to go to the Chinese district. I had lunch in a restaurant on Calle Dragones, and then I walked to Manrique. I remembered the house, I remembered it better than I had expected, I felt excitement, and some tenderness too: I was part of all this, this neighborhood and this house, part of the story of the frigate Oquendo, and of the enlightened journey of Sanfancón. I knocked twice, and an old man in an undershirt opened the door; he had an enormous wart on his nose, and he wore glasses. I asked for Pancho Wong, one of the two men my mother said might still be left of the group who had originally lived with my grandfather. The old man shook his head and said that Pancho had died. Then I asked for Felipe Alam; my mother had said he was one of the younger ones. The old man replied that Felipe was at the laundry. I was silent, thinking I had nobody left to ask for, and then it occurred to me to tell him I was the granddaughter of Yuan Pei Fu and wanted to see his room. He was very surprised and asked me to wait at the door; he didn't come back for several minutes, and when he did he was accompanied by another Chinese, who looked like a phantom: a sack of yellow bones with a bald head and scabs covering his skin.

"Are you Aida?" he asked in a sad, distant voice that sounded like the voice of a drowning man.

"I'm Enriqueta Cheng, Aida's daughter, the granddaughter of Domitila Cuervo."

He led me into the vestibule, and there an Oriental aroma filled the air, a mix of a thousand foul smells and a thousand perfumes. I saw an empty wheelchair and remembered the cripple and his little paper figures. I also remembered Pérez Navarro, who claimed that the cripple was the watchman at an opium den. Almost against my will, I thought of the words Tata Sandoval had said to my mother: the Chinese killed with paper and did their work with dragonflies.

"And so," I said, for the sake of saying something, "Pancho is dead?"

Neither of them answered. They looked at me with curiosity; perhaps they were seeking my grandfather's eyes in mine and were disappointed by the fact that not much of his eyes remained.

My eyes were Enrico Caruso's, and I had also inherited the dimple in his chin.

"I've come to see his room, if that's possible."

The Chinese who looked like a phantom said his name was Roberto Mui and he had never met my grandfather, since he had moved there only ten years ago. I repeated that I wanted to see the room, and he seemed to think about it; he exchanged a glance with the old man who had opened the door for me, and then he simply said "Come." He shuffled along in front of me down the same hallway I had walked with my grandmother years before. He opened the door to the room, which looked exactly the same: a narrow bed, a dresser with a Chinese lantern, a table covered with medallions and bells, and a glass case that held pipes. On the long wall there was still the same immense altar, with candles burned halfway down, placards written in Chinese characters, censers for burning sandalwood, and porcelain vases. In the center of the altar, above the shelf that held dozens of bronze miniatures and paper figures cut out by the cripple, there was a terrible absence, the great void left by the image of Sanfancón.

I walked to the dresser. On it was a tray with very old sticks of incense, a box that looked like jade, and a photograph: it was a picture of my grandmother Domitila, along with my mother and a little girl who wasn't me. I knew right away she was my sister, Baldomero's daughter, who had died not long after her father. I had never seen this photograph; it hadn't been on the dresser the day I came with my grandmother, or when I attended the cripple's wake. Someone had obviously set it there afterward.

"Pancho Wong put it here before he died," said Roberto Mui, as if he knew what I was thinking.

I asked him why Pancho Wong had the photograph, and he replied that my grandmother had given it to him out of friendship, and that my mother had been very fond of him because Pancho was the one who took care of them, bringing them the money sent by Yuan Pei Fu, who was always too busy and couldn't visit very often. Roberto Mui opened a drawer and took out two more photographs: one was of my grandmother Domitila, so young I hardly recognized her, wearing her hair in braids, and the other was of my mother when she was still a little girl. He said these pictures had also belonged to Pancho Wong.

"And this one," he added, showing me a group photograph. "I don't know who they are."

Several men were on the sand. The ocean must have been in front of them because behind them you could see only wooden cabins, with porches and railings and some open doors. Enrico Caruso was at the center of the photograph, dressed all in white and surrounded by five or six men in light clothing, most of them barefoot. On his shoulders, in a kind of joke, Caruso was carrying an old man, and between his spread legs appeared the head of a man with a large handlebar mustache. In a corner was the name of the photographer: "Photo: Kiko" and the year it had been taken: 1920.

"It's a picture of my father," I said to Roberto Mui, and I asked him if I could have it.

"You can have this one," he agreed, after hesitating a few seconds, "but not the ones of your grandmother."

I smiled and thanked him. I gave a final glance at the abandoned altar, the empty hole, without a wisp of smoke, where the image of Sanfancón once had shone. When I was at the door, saying goodbye, Felipe Alam came in, as old as the others but more cordial, with intelligent eyes and a slow, clear way of speaking, something very rare in the Cantonese. He said he remembered seeing me at the wake for Pedro Tan, which was the cripple's name. But I had to confess to him that I barely remembered the paisanos I had met at the wake. He asked for my mother, and I told him she was very ill. And then, just to see how he would react, I said perhaps she would feel better when she saw what I was bringing her: a photograph of my father on the beach. I took out the picture of Caruso and showed it to Felipe Alam, who became very somber and advised me not to show it to her, because she had never known that Yuan Pei Fu had the picture.

"I didn't know it belonged to Yuan Pei Fu," I said.

"It belonged to him, and when he died, Pancho Wong kept it with the other photographs he had of your mother and grandmother. That's why I'm telling you not to show it to your mother; she'll think what isn't so, she'll think Yuan Pei Fu worked that photograph to do harm to your father."

Felipe Alam spoke correct Spanish, unlike the other Chinese. I told him so, and he attributed it to his habit of reading Cuban newspapers and not only papers published in Chinese, which is what most of the other paisanos did.

He asked if I'd like to come in again and have tea, and I said it was after two and I had to be at the radio station by three. But I asked him to please answer just one question: did he know if Yuan Pei Fu had anything to do with the misfortune that occurred in Trinidad?

Felipe Alam pulled back almost involuntarily. He had not been aware that I knew this part of the story. The other two Chinese had disappeared, leaving him and me alone at the door, looking out on the street where all kinds of people passed by, but especially paisanos, who murmured a greeting and looked at the house with veneration.

"Yuan Pei Fu worked with herbs, with birds and other animals," said Felipe Alam. "He could cast a spell on dolls better than anybody. He read the future with mirrors. His protections were swallowed, and he prepared other protections that were like little pillows with cases made of Chinese silk. He was the only one who understood the 'refined' Chinese that the spirits of the ancestors spoke. When one of us got sick, he invoked the spirit of a woman, a very old spirit who would come all the way from China at night and cure us.

"For all these reasons, and because he brought the first image of Sanfancón to Cuba—the image that lit our way when we were so poor and so despairing—when it came time to bury him we buried him with the Six Sacred Objects of Jade, in homage to Heaven, Earth, and the Four Directions: Red Jade, called Chang, at the head *of the corpse to honor the South; White Jade, called Ju, on the right side to honor the West; Gray Jade, called Shi, on the left side to honor the East; Brown Jade, called Tai-Shu, at the feet of a corpse, to honor the North; Green Jade, called Kuei, on the left, to honor Heaven, and Yellow Jade, placed on his belly, to honor Earth. . . . We also opened his mouth and put in pearls and coins to ensure a good journey.*

"Your grandfather did good things and bad things. But what you've mentioned was not one of the bad things. He couldn't travel to Trinidad when what happened happened, he was too old and sick, and he decided to stay at the altar, praying to Sanfancón to save the daughter he loved. But Pancho Wong was in Trinidad—I never knew if Yuan Pei Fu sent him or if he went because he wanted to, because of the great fondness he had for your mother and your grandmother. He went to protect them both: Domitila, who rushed off to Trinidad with the black man Cheché, and your mother—we didn't know if she was alive or dead.

"If people tell you that Yuan Pei Fu had anything to do with the misfortune, don't believe it. They told your mother that, and she never forgave your grandfather. Or didn't forgive him till it was too late, when your grandfather was already dead. That's why you mustn't show her that photograph. I never knew how it came into Yuan Pei Fu's hands, but I can tell you this: by the time it was given to him everything had already happened, your mother was in Havana, your grandmother was taking care of her, and that man, the singer, had left Cuba. You were on the way, and that held Yuan Pei Fu back: he couldn't do anything against your father because he knew anything he did against him would also touch his seed, and that seed was his own granddaughter.

"You're the proof that Yuan Pei Fu didn't work the photograph, he didn't do anything to make that man die like a snake, twisting in his own poison. If others did, if Cheché did, I don't know. But your

grandfather thought of you, he knew you would be a woman filled with curiosity, and he knew something else: he knew you would come to this house one day to learn the truth, and by then everybody would be dead, everybody but me, and I would talk to you at this door, at this hour, on this very day. When she comes, he said to me, tell her this: 'The Messenger of Death, whose name is Chui Chi Lon, is always the messenger of our own hearts.'

"What your grandfather meant is that you cannot struggle against what is yours, against the messenger that is yours. Remember that, and give your mother some peace. When she dies, don't forget to place coins in her mouth, or call me and I'll put them in. She is paisana, a daughter of Yuan Pei Fu, blood of a blood not easily forgotten. Go, and don't forget."

Tu . . . in questa tomba!

A musician died during rehearsal at the Teatro Terry. He was a well-known violinist in Cienfuegos, a young mulatto, that's what Enrico told me. He began to cough while he was playing, then suddenly he stopped playing and stood up, took a few steps toward the exit, and a moment later fell to the floor, coughing even harder and trembling. There was no way to help him: he died right there, and Enrico saw up close the passage of death, the image was burned into his mind, he had to leave the theater and walk for a while in the park. The impresario canceled the rehearsal; it started again a few hours later, after they took the body away. But it wasn't the same because that sorrow was still floating in the air, that grief at seeing a man pass on.

I came back from Palmira when it was almost dark, but nobody asked where I had been, not even Enrico, because he was so troubled: he saw the musician's death as a bad omen for himself. I only told him that everything was arranged for us to run away the next day, and he looked at me as though he didn't know what I was talking about. Then he bowed his head and mumbled that he wasn't sure running away was the best way out for us. I didn't try to persuade him—just the opposite—I didn't say anything for a while, and finally I broke the silence to tell him that if he had changed his mind he ought to say so right away because I had to tell the men who were going to take us to Trinidad.

"Trinidad," he said. "What are we going to do there?"

I told him it was a very isolated place, and almost the only way to get there was by sea. I promised him that in Trinidad, more than anywhere else on earth, we'd be safe. While I talked to him he took deep breaths and rubbed his hands together, and again he said he wasn't sure running away would be a good thing, he wasn't even sure we had to run away at all. I was angry, but I knew how to control myself. I thought this was Enrico's way of telling me that after he sang in Cienfuegos we'd go back to Havana, and from Havana he'd leave for New York, or wherever it was he had to go, and I'd go back to my house on Cruz de Amargura, Cross of Bitterness: that was the full name of my street.

"We'll decide tomorrow," he said, putting his hand on my shoulder. "I have to think about it."

We had supper with Punzo and Zirato, because Mario still didn't feel well and decided to stay in bed. Zirato wanted Enrico to go to a party that some people in Cienfuegos were having, but he refused to go out, he said he didn't want to sweat any more than he was sweating. Supper was very silent, and uncomfortable because of the heat, a suffocating heat that was like an animal: it rested its paws on us and breathed a vapor that stuck to our skin. I had the feeling that the shadow of something, or someone, was with us that night, and the feeling grew even stronger when Enrico complained he was getting a headache. Zirato asked me if I could prepare cold compresses to put over his eyes, that was one of the few things that brought him relief. Then, when I was preparing the compresses, Punzo came into the kitchen and we had the only friendly conversation I remember between him and me: he said Enrico often suffered from splitting headaches, and it was important for him to be better by the next day because singing when he had the pain destroyed him. Since I didn't know anything about opera, he told me part of the story we were going to see: in the story Enrico was named

Rodolpho and he fell in love with a woman they called Mimí, a little thing who always had cold hands.

I thanked Punzo and went to Enrico's room, he was lying down with his clothes on and all he wanted was to keep his eyes closed. I put the compresses over his eyes and fanned him with my sandalwood fan. I don't know if it was the perfumed air, or the cold cloths on his head, but whatever it was, he grew much calmer, and without opening his eyes he took my hand, stroked it with the same tenderness he showed when we first met, and admitted he'd reserved a cabin on the steamship *Cartago*, that was the ship we'd sail on from Havana. He said he had decided to take me with him to New York, and I'd live in a hotel until he took care of all his engagements and we could leave for Naples.

I tried to be happy about the news, and I was, in a way. But I also had my *aché*, my ability to see the other face of life, the broth of uncertainty and mystery where the will of man is always floating. My heart told me that nothing Enrico was saying would happen. It was a premonition, a vision that came to me from inside. That's what it means to have *aché*, and the person who has it knows what I'm talking about. I leaned over him and rubbed his temples, I put a drop of saliva between my fingers: that's what I had seen Calazán do when he wanted to bring down blood pressure. And though I was dying to tell him that he should forget about the steamship *Cartago*, that we should run away to Trinidad, I closed my mouth and didn't tell him anything.

The next morning he was cured. Before he left for the rehearsal he said he wouldn't be back for lunch but I should be ready by six. That's when he'd send somebody to bring me to the theater. I watched him go out with Mario and Punzo; Zirato had already left. As soon as I was alone, I got ready to go back to

Pueblo Grifo and tell Tata Sandoval that we weren't going to Trinidad, and ask him to thank Nicolás Iznaga for me and say I would never forget the favor he was willing to do for me.

I dressed slowly, I didn't like the way anything looked because I was beginning to realize this might be the last night I'd spend with Enrico. I wanted somebody to throw the *ékuele* for me and read the chain and tell me the direction my life was going to take. I needed to know if that direction included the sign that meant the ocean, travel on a ship, happiness on the *Cartago*, the steamship I never saw, not even in my dreams. I was so nervous I put my hat on backward, I looked in the mirror and was struck by what I saw: with my hair pulled up on top of my head, I looked like one of those Chinese women on the calendars that came from Canton. Noro Cheng, the man who wasn't my father but still gave me his name, was fascinated by those calendars. He had piles of them in his laundry, and he also brought them home and hung them over the bed. I think in his heart he dreamed about those silent paisanas, dreamed about going to Canton to find a wife of his own race and make up for all the years he'd had to settle for a dark-skinned woman, which was all he could hope for in Cuba.

Before I left I went to the kitchen for a glass of water, and Asteria, the maid I got on with so well, said I should have lemonade instead. You see, Enriqueta, we carry coincidences in our blood, we attract them like lightning. I didn't even have time to raise the glass to my mouth, because just then the door slammed and Enrico came in. His face was red and he was breathing with his mouth open—he looked as frightened as the day we met in the Hotel Inglaterra. He gave the servant a worried look and asked me to go with him, he had to talk to me. I went with him, thinking the worst, thinking he'd ask me to leave the house or go back to Havana right away.

"Are you sure everything's arranged?" He grabbed my shoulders and shook me, and I was too confused to say anything. "That trip," he insisted, "are you sure nobody knows about it?"

Beads of sweat rolled down his forehead. I've never forgotten Enrico's eyes at that moment, or the way he moved his mouth, how he gasped for air.

"Those who have to know about it know about it," I said. "But that's the same as nobody knowing."

"We're going," he said. "There's nothing else for me to do."

Then he told me he'd been threatened again, an anonymous letter had been given to the porter at the Teatro Terry. The police were watching the area, they were certain another bomb could explode there, and if they didn't kill him inside the theater, there was always the possibility they'd try on the train: it was a long way from Cienfuegos to Havana, leagues and leagues of track, hours of passing through thick woods. The worst might happen to him on the train.

I took off my hat, and I think I began to look like the Chinese women on the calendars again. I started to kiss Enrico, and each kiss dampened my lips with his sweat. I told him not to worry, that a Congo brotherhood would help us; he didn't know what that was, but I would explain it to him: a brotherhood was like a family in a house, a group of people who'd taken a blood oath to help each other. No man made a move, no animal took a step, not a soul could hide without one of them knowing. They knew all the tricks, all the twists and turns, all the hiding places.

I believe I finally calmed him. I told him Nicolás Iznaga's plan, and I asked him for money. We decided to keep everything a secret till the end, so he changed his clothes and went back to the rehearsal. At six o'clock sharp a horse-drawn carriage came for me. It was decorated with flowers: that was the tradition in

Cienfuegos when you went to the theater. I followed Iznaga's instructions and left a suitcase with Asteria, it had my clothes and Enrico's, and his cigarettes and cologne, and the money we needed to pay for our first expenses and for the boat that would take us to Trinidad. Asteria had been told to give the suitcase to a messenger from the brotherhood, he'd come for it after I left.

Punzo was waiting for me at the door of the theater, and he took me to a box. He had his high-and-mighty attitude back again, he pretended he didn't hear my questions, and when I said we should go and see Enrico, he answered that it was impossible, some reporters were with him and the impresarios didn't allow outside women to visit the performers. I knew it was just an excuse, a lie so he wouldn't have to take me, but instead of insisting I settled into my box and put on a resigned face. It was early and nobody was in the theater; all you heard were sounds behind the curtain, the scraping of furniture being pushed back and forth, the music of just one instrument, I think it was a flute, that kept practicing the same melody over and over again.

I took out my fan: it was like my salvation, something I could hold on to while I was all alone in that totally strange place. After a while the audience began to come in, and I passed the time looking at the elegant ladies of Cienfuegos. I loved their perfume. I'd never been anywhere like this, never been with such distinguished people. Some of them were staring at me, they were surprised to see a Chinese mulatta, without jewels or beautiful clothes, sitting in such an important seat to watch the opera. The lights went out and suddenly the stage was lit. The orchestra began to play, but the curtain hadn't gone up yet when somebody come into my box. At first I thought it was Tata Sandoval, because he was just like him: tall and skinny, with the look of a tailor. But then I realized it was an old man with very fine manners, a man with white skin and tortoiseshell glasses. He asked if I was Señora Aida, and I said I was. Then he whispered: "Come with me. Nicolás Iznaga is waiting for you." I said it must be a mistake: the opera hadn't begun yet, we weren't supposed to leave until the performance was over. His manners didn't change, but his voice was harsh: "Nicolás wants you to come now."

For a moment I didn't know what to do. The old man stayed there, urging me to go, and I thought I had no choice, I had to follow him. I stood as the curtain went up, and I did catch a glimpse of Enrico, wearing a false beard and mustache and rubbing his hands together, the same hands that set me on fire when we were alone together, but in this story they couldn't even warm up the fingers of that girl Mimí; nothing could.

We walked across the empty lobby and left the theater. When we were on the sidewalk, the old man told me to go to a car waiting on the other side of the street. I did what he said and saw that inside the car a man in a hat was signalling for me to get in: it was hard for me to recognize Nicolás Iznaga.

"The performance just started. We can't leave now," I said.

"We're going on ahead," he answered in a hard voice. "They'll bring him later."

He gave an order to the driver, and we drove away slowly. I was afraid the whole thing was a trick; that Asteria, Tata Sandoval, and Iznaga himself had fooled me. I was terrified they were taking me away from Enrico, that my plan was only part of a bigger plan, a trap that had been set long before we ever got to Cienfuegos.

"We're going to Las Minas." Iznaga said, "That's where the boat leaves from."

I didn't answer. I held tight to my fan; it was the only thing I could do. We got to the port, where another man was waiting for us. He was a bowlegged black, I'm sure he was a Congo man, and he took us straight to a hut that was on the edge of the ocean.

Iznaga pointed to a stool: "Sit down, we'll wait for them to bring him."

The door was partly open, and through it you could see a kind of dark schooner.

"That's where you'll be going."

The hours went by. Iznaga and the other man chewed tobacco and walked along the dock. I fanned myself, I stood up and walked in circles, I sat down and loosened my hair, I combed it with my fingers and pinned it up again, that's what I did all that time, and I also rubbed my hands together, they were the only thing I could offer Enrico: living, sinful hands that didn't freeze so easily. At last I heard noises outside, and Iznaga signaled to me not to move. The two of them were quiet, spitting their tobacco juice and watching the car coming closer and closer.

"He's here," Iznaga said finally. "Get in the boat."

I went outside, frantic, afraid it wasn't true. I looked at the car and saw Enrico get out, all wrapped up in the hat and scarf that belonged to the character Rodolpho. I ran to him, threw my arms around his overcoat: lucky for him it was a lightweight coat. Iznaga told us to hurry, the schooner was ready to leave. I helped Enrico take off some of those clothes, and we tossed everything on deck; the suitcase I had left with Asteria was there too. Enrico seemed calm. He looked very different that night: he was still wearing the false mustache, and I thought he was happy to escape.

"First you'll go to Jagua," we heard Iznaga's voice whispering. "The motorboat will be waiting there; it'll take you over to Trinidad."

He turned and got into the car. The bowlegged man took the wheel of the schooner and said we were leaving. I watched the coast of Cienfuegos move away, and I felt happy about escaping, too, a feeling of freedom I'd never had before. As we crossed the bay, Enrico told me that at the end of the performance he'd managed to lose Punzo and Zirato, but Mario had been waiting for him at one of the exits from the stage. When the two men sent by Iznaga came over to him, Mario ran in between and Enrico had to tell him to get away. But his servant wouldn't listen to him, he knew something strange was going on, he grabbed the arm of one of the men, who wheeled around and punched him. In the confusion the other people who were watching the scene, including the impresario from Cienfuegos, couldn't even move or shout. They took Enrico out by the back door of the theater, and very few people on the street even noticed him.

"This is Jagua," the pilot interrupted. "You get off here."

The schooner had anchored near shore, and we waited in the dark for a boat to come alongside.

"Bring on the Havañeros!" somebody shouted from the boat, and I answered with the second part of the password:

"We're on our way!"

We jumped into the boat, and it took us to the beach. Jagua was a quiet village; it had a castle, but all we could see was its outline. The man from the boat lit our way with a kerosene lamp, he led us along a path, and our shoes kept sinking into the sand. A wooden bridge was at the end of the path, and there we finally saw the motorboat: it was waiting for us with the engine running.

Our guide raised the lantern: "That old tub's for you."

We climbed aboard and didn't even see the face of the man who would steer it. I made sure they had brought our suitcase. I noticed it was damp and prayed the dampness hadn't seeped into our clothes or the cigarettes, dozens of the packs that Enrico depended on to live. The trip took more than three hours, and Enrico smoked the whole time, not saying a word. We sat on a worm-eaten bench and he held on to me—he didn't let go even when we saw some lights and the shape of the mountains around Trinidad.

A car was waiting for us on the beach at La Boca. It must have been two or three in the morning. The streets were empty, and I was afraid the noise would wake people and they'd look out to see who was going by. The car stopped in front of a simple house with iron grilles and shutters, just like all the other houses around it. As soon as we got out, the door opened, and we saw a skinny black girl who greeted us with old words: "Good evening to you, Master, Mistress." The heat had followed us, and Trinidad was like an oven filled with shadows and phantoms. We took off our shoes—they were full of sand—we drank a whole pitcher of orange juice, and we got into bed when the roosters began to crow. Enrico didn't bother to check the sheets, he didn't even ask if they were linen—of course they weren't— or if they were absolutely clean, that was something that always worried him. Since his escape he was a different person, as though some witchcraft had created a deep canyon between the man who ran away from Cienfuegos at night and the one who reached Trinidad before dawn.

No matter what people said afterward, I didn't put a spell on Enrico. It's hard for me to talk about these things now, but I swear to God I didn't do anything to bind him, there was no *ayé*, no *morubba*. . . . I didn't give him anything to drink; I didn't cut his nails or work the hair from his belly or steal his fluids, not his sweat, not his semen. All I did was take him inside me, but it was his will, he sank into this Chinese flesh because he wanted to, this flesh that turned mulatta when we made love. He clung to me in a spiritual way: it had something to do with what happened to us on the trip. Remember, the whole trip was on water, and water is my element, the kingdom of Yemayá, the place where I cast out but also gather in. On the ocean, on that quiet night, all the Chinese phantoms awoke, all the ghosts from the steamship *Oquendo;* and the black phantoms, all the ones who came with my grandmother Petrona of the Lucumi nation. There was a power, a great gathering, many *egungún* hovering around—they're the dead playing their tricks. I felt it in the air: it was a night of fire and war, and when I was in bed I could feel the thirst of those spirits, their wandering back and forth—you can feel that in your hair, it's like a feather passing over your head—their movements and their bumping, demanding the glass of water that brings them relief. In my sleep I was tempted to get up and put out water for them and get them to leave me alone. But I was so tired I couldn't even open my eyes.

When the spirits grew quiet, Enrico gave a start in bed. First he shouted, and then I knew he was talking in his sleep. There wasn't much light, and I could just make out his face. It was covered with sweat—that was nothing new—but it was also twisted by his nightmare.

I shook him and he opened his eyes, but I didn't know if he saw me.

"I dreamed about my funeral," he said.

I took a handkerchief and wiped his forehead.

"And me," I asked him, "did you happen to see me in the grave?"

I'd be lying if I said I wasn't afraid. I was shivering inside, but he went back to sleep, and for the first time in many days I thought he was resting, that he found contentment in his sleep. Bells rang, and the village started to wake up. I heard horses' hooves, the calls of fishwives, the sound of bottles clinking against each other, the crying of some children, or maybe it was only one. When it was morning I got up and went to the kitchen. I found the black girl boiling milk: she looked at me again with respect and came out with the same phrase she had said the night before: "Good day to you, Mistress." I dressed and went to buy bread. It was the first time I'd seen Trinidad in the light of day, and that was when I learned the name of the street where we were staying: Calle del Desengaño, the Street of Disappointment.

In the afternoon, Enrico and I went for a walk. The people were curious about us because they knew we weren't from Trinidad, but that didn't mean they took Enrico for a foreigner. No, he looked like the owner of a sugar mill, a landowner from Sancti Spiritus, with his Panama hat and linen trousers and two-tone shoes: white stitching on the black, and black stitching on the white. We bought tobacco from the cigar makers in the arcade, we drank sweet wine in a cantina near the port. I watched Enrico out of the corner of my eye, I saw him smoking while he looked at the view, and it was hard for me to recognize the sick, tormented man I had met in Havana. We lived that glory for a couple of days.

Afterward, I never wanted to go back to Trinidad because I didn't want to die of the memory: I knew that if I went back there I'd faint in the street; I knew very well I couldn't endure the nostalgia or the horror. Because there was horror, Enriqueta, horror and blood.

I'll tell it all to you. It's all I have to leave you.

I hadn't thought about them until that Sunday in November when I opened the door and saw them standing there, asking if they could see my mother.

María Vigil and Amable Casanova came to the house together a little after ten in the morning, and by the expression on their faces and the way they were dressed, I knew they wanted to say goodbye to the woman who had been their friend for so many years: Aida Petrirena Cheng, mortally wounded by cancer.

I told them my mother was still sleeping, and they said they would wait until she woke, if I didn't mind. I replied that on the contrary, this would give us a chance to talk, and I asked them to have a seat and offered them coffee. They both looked at me with curiosity, because although they had known me since I was a little girl, we hadn't seen one another for quite some time. It may have been years since I'd seen María Vigil. She was over seventy, much older than my mother, and she had also been a friend and client of my grandmother's. And yet María Vigil had what is called a shady past, and from that past she still carried a nickname famous throughout Cuba: Macorina. I once asked my mother how it was possible that my grandmother, who was such a respectable woman, had allowed Macorina to visit her house and become friends with her daughter. My mother's answer was that María Vigil had always been a discreet person who went out of her way to help other people and had a talent for showing up just when she was most needed. She remembered that on the day I was born, María had come with the midwife and hadn't left her side, encouraging her to push. Later on, it was her idea to name me Enriqueta, an idea my grandmother didn't like at first, though it pleased my mother very much.

That Sunday in November, as I watched her sipping coffee, I looked at María Vigil as I never had before. She had a bony face and prominent cheekbones and wore her hair pulled back in a bun; she was very gray by now, but I seemed to remember that as a younger woman she had been blond. People said Macorina had abandoned her wild ways at the age of forty, when she fell in love with a married man who repaired typewriters. For years, until he died, he would go to Macorina's house early each morning with his damaged machines and repair them there, on her dining room table, while she prepared his lunch. In the afternoon he would gather up his tools, deliver the machines he had repaired, and return to his real house, where he lived with his wife.

Amable Casanova, on the other hand, had led a much quieter life. She was my mother's age, perhaps a few years younger, the widow of a merchant seaman with whom she'd had no children. Recently she had been courted by a Dominican friar from the Convent of San Juan de Letrán. About the time my mother fell ill, she would come to our house for advice as to whether or not she should accept the Dominican, who had promised to hang up his habit as soon as Amable said yes. She wasn't a pretty woman, but she had one of those bodies that could easily arouse a priest: large breasts that almost always overflowed her neckline, the hips of an old-fashioned laundress, and her gray streak, a streak like a warning light in her black, wavy hair.

While my mother slept, I brought them up-to-date regarding her real condition. I told them that nobody knew exactly how much longer she would live, but the doctor doubted she'd see the new year. Both of them turned pale, María Vigil's eyes filled with tears, and she said she never thought my mother would die before her.

"If she survived Trinidad," she whispered, looking down at the floor, "I would have thought she could survive anything."

Amable Casanova gave a start and looked at me in dismay. My mother had surely let them know she was telling me the truth, but they had no way of knowing how far along she was in her story, or which details I knew and which ones she was going to keep from me, perhaps forever.

"She's telling me everything," I said, trying to seem unperturbed. "Yesterday she began to talk about Trinidad."

Amable wanted María Vigil's support, and she looked at her before she would reveal anything to me, but María continued to stare at the floor.

"Sometimes she repeats certain things," I added, preparing the ground for the opportunity I now had to persuade the two women to talk to me. "I don't know if it's because she's sick, but she mixes up dates and forgets certain names. I'm writing everything down, I plan to put it all in order."

María Vigil raised her head. "Why do you want to put it in order?"

"I want to know what happened to them," I said, "I want to know why my father didn't give me his name or ever come to see me."

"You know he had a wife," Amable whispered, "an American wife, and a little girl."

"Besides," said María, "how could he come to see you if he died so soon? That was the problem, Enriqueta, you were just a baby, only a few weeks or a couple of months old when he died."

Amable looked into my eyes; she was a woman with tremendous powers of sight. According to my mother, who had known her since she was a girl, Amable had the ability to see the future in aquamarines, the blue stones. And if she set her mind to it, she could also see the future in a yellow topaz.

"I don't know what Aída's told you," Amable said. "I do know she was going to tell you everything, or almost everything. There are some things you shouldn't expect anybody to tell you. They're very intimate, and there's no reason for you to know them."

We spoke very quietly, we were careful not to let my mother hear us in her bedroom. María Vigil had taken out a handkerchief and was drying her eyes. I moved my chair over to the sofa, where they were sitting, and spoke to them in a confidential tone; perhaps I couldn't hide what I wanted:

"I'm writing down everything she says in one notebook, and in another I write what other people tell me, those who knew her back then, and those who knew my father. I've also talked to people who were in the theater the day the bomb exploded."

"The bomb!" exclaimed María Vigil. "My God, that was 1920!"

Amable Casanova leaned forward. "Do you want to write down what I tell you?"

It surprised me to hear her say that, but I nodded and went to find my notebook.

Write this down, Enriqueta: that worn-out Chinese woman lying in bed isn't your mother. Your mother was a beauty; she didn't look Cuban but she wasn't an ordinary Chinese either. She was like a picture, just as if somebody came and painted her. Your mother was painted, who knows, probably that mystical Chinaman who was her real father painted her too. Yuan Pei Fu was a crafty brujo who owned a lot of businesses, but I remember that he adored your mother, and so did Noro Cheng, who was her father for the sake of appearances.

I'll tell you this, Calazán saw it all in the ékuele in January, but I saw it long before that. I saw it in an aquamarine my husband brought back from one of his voyages. Seeing into stones isn't easy. You have to keep your eyes fixed on the jewel for more than five minutes, and you have to do it with your mind blank. Sometimes your eyes fill with tears, and then you have to stop right away. When the stone's ready to open—that's what it's called when the stone's going to show you the future—then a kind of mist comes out of the aquamarine, a smoke like wine; it gives you the feeling that the stone is turning to liquid. And in that liquid all things are seen. I saw your mother there, and though you may not believe it, I saw the baby girl that was you in her arms. At that time we didn't even dream that Enrico Caruso would sing in Havana. But I saw him *too, in the smoke and debris, and I saw, just like I'm seeing you now, the son of a bitch who set the bomb. I always knew who did it.*

I remember that on the afternoon I saw everything, I ran out of my house and came here. Your grandmother was sewing, poor thing, she was always sewing, and your mother was taking a bath. Before I got here I knew she'd be taking a bath. Your grandmother had her abilities too, and from the minute she laid eyes on me she knew I'd seen something that scared me. She stood up and walked toward me. "What is it, Amable?" I shook my head. "I don't know, Domitila: did something blow up?" I didn't tell her you were coming because then she'd think Aida was pregnant, and that wasn't true. You were in the air; even though you wouldn't be in your mother's belly for months, you made your presence known. Some babies make their presence known before they're conceived.

Enrico Caruso went wild over Aida. She says they met in the kitchen of the Hotel Inglaterra, but I think it happened in the theater, a few days before the bomb went off. She never wanted to admit she'd been at the theater, though it was something she did very often: she went there to watch the elegant ladies going to the opera; she'd look at the dresses they were wearing, and later she'd copy them on paper. She and your grandmother would make them exactly the same, they had clients who paid a lot of money for their copies.

Maybe she was near the theater when he came there and that's when he fell for her. It wasn't easy for any man to see a woman like your mother and keep on walking. Least of all Caruso: everybody knew that women were his weakness.

The bomb exploded in the middle of June. A neighbor stopped by to tell me, she said people were dead and injured in the theater. And it came to me like a bolt out of the blue that Aida was involved in this. My husband was at sea, I was alone in the house and didn't dare to leave at that time of night to find out. I waited till the next morning, I came to this house bright and early, and the first thing your grandmother said to me was this: "What had to explode exploded." I asked her if your mother was all right, and she said yes, but that she was in Regla with José de Calazán. Then I remember that your grandmother asked me to sit down, she said I was like part of the family, like a sister to her daughter, and to show how much she trusted me she was going to confess something very serious: "Aida's in Regla with that man, the one called Caruso." Then she begged me to tell her the rest, she thought I had seen other things in the aquamarine. I didn't want to tell her about you, but her eyes were full of tears: she said Calazán had seen a lot of blood, and your grandfather, Aida's real father, had seen something terrible in the smoke of Sanfancón. I felt sorry for her, there were tears in my eyes too, I felt a weight on my conscience. "I didn't see blood, Domitila, I swear I didn't." She took my hand. "And if you didn't see blood, Amable, tell me this: what is it you don't want to say to me?" I couldn't keep it quiet anymore, and I told her: I admitted I had seen Aida holding a baby, she was bound to end up pregnant.

Your grandmother became very thoughtful. She said she had always wanted Aida to have another baby to make up for the daughter she had lost, but now she was afraid the baby would come at a bad time or that she'd have it with the wrong person. "Tell me if Caruso's the father," she said. "The man's on his last legs. Calazán knows that and he's trying to keep him from dying in Cuba."

I swore I didn't know anything else and said I didn't plan to look into the aquamarine again because it terrified me. I left and didn't return to this house until your mother came back from Trinidad, she was the one who sent for me.

You shouldn't tell her what I've told you. I don't know what you know, but it seemed to me you had to know this, at least.

I thanked her and got up to see if my mother was awake. I tiptoed into her room and found her with her eyes open. I said good morning

and told her that María Vigil and Amable Casanova were waiting to
see her. She asked me to help her get up and get dressed, and she complained about my not waking her earlier.

When she was ready, I went back to the living room and found
the two women talking quietly. I told them they could go in to see my
mother and that I'd be in the kitchen preparing breakfast. Amable
stood up right away, but María Vigil stayed where she was, looking
me up and down. Abruptly she got to her feet, followed me into the
kitchen, and smoothed my hair with her hand.

I don't know how to look into aquamarines, Enriqueta, I don't have
that ability. But I have something else: a good deal of experience. In
1920 I was old compared to your mother. And I had retired, if you
take my meaning. You know who I am, your mother must have told
you, and if she didn't, people on the street know who Macorina is.
That name was never mentioned here; your grandmother always
called me María, and so did your mother, and from the time you
were a baby it was the only name for me you knew. And because of
that, because I've always loved the women in this house, I'm going
to tell you something: your mother never regretted her romance with
Caruso, and he probably didn't regret it either. He did things for her
that a man doesn't do unless he's really in love. I saw them in Regla,
I went with your grandmother to Cheché's house—that's what we
called Calazán. I stayed outside, waiting for your grandmother to
talk to your mother. Calazán came out to see me. I was almost forty
years old but I still was a little frightened to be with that man. You
see, Calazán had wanted me many years earlier, when he was a
young babalawo and I was in my prime. Somebody told me that
Calazán wanted to bind me. I was blond and white-skinned, and he
began to say that he'd have me, that he'd prepared the afoché, the
powders that would make me give in. For years I was scared to
death, but nothing happened, no spell did me harm, because I

always had my good protection with me. Yuan Pei Fu himself prepared that protection for me, and I had to swallow it in his presence because you swallow the protections of the Chinese babalawos and then nobody can do anything against them. The day I went with your grandmother to Regla, Calazán came over to me, smooth as silk, and said I should go in, nobody ate people in his house. I said I preferred to stay outside, I knew the atmosphere inside was very charged. Then I asked about Aida, and he said he was taking care of her, and I asked about Caruso, and he said he couldn't take care of him because he was dead and only Oyá can take care of the dead. He said he wouldn't trespass on the saints, he wasn't going to fight with the orishas over a man that Ikú was already holding by the hand.

Then he invited me to see Caruso while he was sleeping. We walked around to the back of the house and looked through a window. It was the first and last time I saw your father. He was naked, he had a white cloth across his forehead, he was fat and half bald, and his whole body was covered in sweat. A fly had landed on his face, and others were buzzing around him. Calazán put his hand on my back: "He's ready to go, but I don't want him to go while he's with my goddaughter." I asked him if Caruso was sick, and he said it wasn't that he was sick but that he'd been marked, and that was worse than being sick. He ran his hand down my back to my bottom and said: "Macorina, damn it, I stood on my head to bind you." I burst out laughing: "Old man, can't you see I ate Chinese protection, and nobody can do anything against Chinese witchcraft?"

I was happy because it just so happened that on the day the bomb exploded—that was a Sunday—there was a knock at my door and when I opened it I saw a skinny man, well dressed with his sparkling clean shirt and nice straw hat. He had a mustache and talked very properly; you could tell he was educated. He asked if anyone had called from my house to have a typewriter fixed. I told him there was no typewriter here, but maybe it was next door, a notary lived there. He stood there looking at me, as though he didn't have the heart to leave. He was younger than me, no more than thirty or thirty-two years old, and he was sweating: that summer of 1920 was the hottest summer I can remember. And because it was so hot, I asked him in for a lemonade.

It surprised me that he was working on Sunday, and I told him so. He said that during the week he went to businesses, and on Sundays he repaired the typewriters of notaries and other people who worked at home. At that moment I heard knocking on the window. I looked out, and somebody on the street shouted that there had been an explosion at the Teatro Nacional and everybody inside was dead. When he heard that, the man put down his lemonade and stood up. I saw that he intended to leave and I told him not to, in case there was another explosion. He sat down again, and that was my good fortune.

When I went to Regla the next day with your grandmother, I was more excited about him than I had been about anybody for a long time, and if I hadn't been so worried over what was happening to your mother, I would have blessed the explosion. From then on, Angelito Capiró—that was his name—began to visit me every day and bring his work so he could do it in my house. He was the most considerate man, he was never any trouble, he'd sit down to do his repairs and ask me for some coffee. The months went by, and then March came; I was very concerned about your mother and often visited this house. One morning your grandmother sent word to the midwife to come right away, and the midwife, who was a good friend of mine, stopped by my house to tell me. We came here together, and I watched you being born; it looked like an easy birth to me but your mother had a lot of pain. When I got back home, so tired of pushing with Aida, Angelito was waiting for me. I told him you had been born—he already knew the story, he knew you were

Caruso's daughter. He asked me what your name was and I told him you didn't have a name yet. And then, since he was so educated, he said they ought to give you an operatic name. I wrote down the names that occurred to him: Adina, Santuzza, Nedda, and others that were even stranger. I told him your mother wasn't going to give you any of those names, especially Santuzza, nobody in Cuba would dare to use a name like that. He put his arms around me: "Well, it doesn't matter, love; they should call her Enriqueta, so she'll have something of her father's."

And the next day I came here with that idea. Maybe you wouldn't have his last name for a while, but at least you'd have the first. Nobody could take that from you.

Angelito knew you when you were little. You don't remember, but he used to call you Enrica, Carusita, Carusela, and names he got from operas; you liked to repeat them. Years later he died suddenly in his house just as he was getting ready to come to mine. I found out a few days afterward, when his wife had already buried him.

I cried for him like a madwoman and mourned him like a widow. He was the great love the bomb brought to me. That was the day Macorina died.

Ciel!...Aïda

*T*here was a time when the brujas of Trinidad, who weren't black women like the ones in Cárdenas but white brujas from the Canary Islands, would gather together and celebrate their festivals on the slope of La Vigía. They would go up at night and come down at dawn, and along the trail they scattered a powder that smelled of fish. People breathed it in and got sick with rashes, or they went blind; the children had convulsions: they would fall down, stiff as boards, their hands clenched tight.

I heard this story many years later when you, Enriqueta— you were always a great reader—brought home a book and showed me a drawing of Trinidad. You must have been thirteen or fourteen. I know for a fact that nobody had told you about what your parents went through there, but for some mysterious reason the tower attracted your attention, it was the convent tower, and then you wanted me to read the story about the brujas, you kept talking about the caves: "Caniquí," you said, "the Cave of Caniquí," and when I heard that I became so frightened, it was the sort of spasm that travels up your chest and fills your mouth with fear and calamity.

On the morning of our second day in Trinidad, I asked Enrico to walk with me along the beach. I stopped at a stand on the street and bought some nougat, the kind made with cashews, it helps relieve nausea. He was smoking and didn't want to eat, but I did; I didn't know yet I was pregnant and I was beginning to get those yens, a yen to eat nougat or drink sugarcane juice. Sweet things were all I wanted.

While we were walking I smelled that fishy odor: not the odor of fresh fish, that smell that's a little like the smell of the ocean, but something else, like the odor in a food store, something oily and buried in salt. I didn't see any dust floating in the air, or maybe I didn't look, but Enrico complained that his eyes were burning, and my arms began to itch. We felt better as soon as we were on the beach. Nobody else was there. We sat for a while on the sand, and Enrico wanted to go in the water: he took off his shirt and rolled up his trousers, and he went swimming in front of me; I stayed on shore. Then he said he had been swallowing sea water on purpose, because swallowing it was very good for his throat.

At noon we walked back to the house. For the first time since we came to Trinidad, Enrico mentioned Mario and Zirato. He didn't talk about the others, but in a quiet voice he said he didn't even want to imagine the commotion going on now in Havana, and maybe in New York; they must have heard by now about his disappearance. He lowered his eyes, and as he walked he looked down at the ground, at the streets paved with stones from the river and clay bricks: with that combination some footsteps echoed but not others. I'm sure he was thinking about his American wife and his little girl, and maybe about his family in Naples. Before we got to the house he asked me if I'd heard anything from the brotherhood. I said it was still too soon, but in a few days they'd let us know when it was time to go back to Havana, and they'd do it by way of the black girl who cooked for us, she was our go-between with Nicolás Iznaga.

While we ate lunch we planned an outing: we had seen a park with a wrought-iron pavilion, and somebody told us a band would play there that night. After lunch we had a siesta. It was more Enrico's habit than mine, but that afternoon we both were exhausted. I thought it was because of our exercise on the beach, and also the fish odor, that rancid smell, had stayed in our nostrils. Enrico lay down first, and I staggered after him. I fell into bed and sank into a kind of half-sleep that was like half-cooked soup: I could see light and hear sounds, but at the same time I couldn't move. I remember that at one point I felt desperate because I wanted to wake up but couldn't; I sobbed in my sleep, and Enrico must have heard me sobbing, but he couldn't wake up either. Hours went by like this, it wasn't normal, we didn't sleep that long because we wanted to.

It was dark when I finally opened my eyes again. The lamp in the room was lit, and the first thing I saw was the figure of a man standing in front of me. It all happened very fast: the man came at me—he was a heavyset mulatto—and it was all I could do to get out of his way. I screamed and jumped out of bed; I don't know if Enrico was awake. I tried to get to the door but couldn't: the man held me against his body and put his hand over my mouth. I felt as though I was choking, and I began to kick and tried to bite his hand, I managed to turn my head for a moment and saw that another man had come into the room and was struggling with Enrico. It moved from struggling to punching, and then I couldn't see anything else because I was dragged into the living room. The windows were open, and the girl who took care of the house watched everything from the door with terrified eyes, hunching over in fear. As I went past the table I managed to grab a glass, I tried to break it in the man's face, but he pushed me against the wall and the glass broke in my hand. A piece of glass sliced my fingers; they weren't cut off right away, but later they had to amputate them: these three, that's when I lost them.

They pulled me out of the house and put me in a car. I didn't know if anybody on the street saw us, I didn't have a voice to scream with, all the struggling and the pain made me feel faint and then my body went limp, I let myself fall, I wanted to die and had the feeling I was getting my wish. It was a nice fall: a moment of peace in all that madness. I think it's what they call resignation.

I almost passed out; my head was hanging down. That's why I didn't see the man's face again, and he never said a word to me. I don't know what his voice was like, or what kind of accent he had; whether he was a foreigner or not is something I can't tell you. After a while the car stopped and they made me get out. I couldn't stand, so the man picked me up and started to carry me. We were in the middle of the countryside, and I heard the nighttime noises: the crickets and night birds. I thought about my mother and Noro Cheng; he was my father on paper and, I realized it only then, he was also my father in my heart. Without wanting to I thought about Baldomero and our little girl, and I thought about my grandmother. I was so confused I thought all those dead were around me and walking with me. I don't even know how long that man carried me. The only thing I could remember later was that the road went up and down, and even so he knew the way and didn't need a light.

I closed my eyes and didn't open them again until we stopped. The smell was different, the country noises had stopped and there were other noises, I couldn't make anything out but when the man started walking again he moved very slowly, like he was having trouble finding his way or keeping his balance. And then he gave up, or reached the spot where he planned to leave me anyway: he just dumped me on the ground, pushed me against a wall, and disappeared. I leaned my head back and discovered that the wall was very damp, it was rock, sharp and rough, and little pools of water were all around me. I realized I was in a cave.

For all these years I've tried to remember what I did that night, and I can't. I know I didn't faint even though I lost so much blood because of my cut fingers. I also know I didn't sleep. But those hours were erased from my mind, as if another spirit had taken the place of mine and was living what I was supposed to live. Years later my mother told me she had the idea I'd spent the night "mounted," possessed by the mistress of my head, that's the saint I'm devoted to. Yemayá is one, but she has seven paths. She can be the messenger of Olokun and stir up muddy waters, then she's called Yemayá Asesu; or she can be the minister of Olofi and wander the tunnels of a cave, and then she's Yemayá Achabá. I don't know which one stayed with me, fighting off everything that was around me: insects of the damp and vipers of death, bats and leeches. I still ask myself why they didn't eat me, why they didn't come into my belly and eat you.

When I was myself again, some rays of light were coming in the entrance to the cave. I could hardly feel my legs—they were numb—but I thought about dragging myself outside. These thoughts came and went, but I was so weak they never got strong enough for me to make a decision or tell my muscles to do anything. I raised my hand; it was beginning to burn. In the dim light I could see the fingers hanging, little pieces of flesh that weren't mine anymore and didn't feel anything for me anymore. I begin to cry, not for my fingers but for Enrico. I thought about the tragedy in my life, and about his death. I supposed my mother would never know where my bones were lying, and not even Calazán or Yuan Pei Fu would be able to help her find them.

The next thing I knew, somebody was shaking me, somebody was shouting my name. At least two men helped me to my feet. I don't know if anybody else was in the cave—everything was blurred—and I didn't recognize the man who picked me up and carried me out of there. He walked a long way before I realized it was Nicolás Iznaga.

We went back to Trinidad. It was like a dream. They took me out of the car and brought me into the house; it was full of blacks. In the living room they sat me in a rocking chair and gave me a cup of café con leche, but I didn't want anything to drink. Just the opposite: I brought up the liquid that was in my stomach, the water I had licked off the walls of the cave. I couldn't stop retching, and I vomited into my own lap. Then a black woman came over to me, she held my head and blew into my face, she sprayed me with rum. I revived a little, enough to lift my hand and be terrified at the sight of those stumps, the dried blood, the ragged ends that nobody had the courage to pull off once and for all.

Nicolás Iznaga stood in front of me.

"I sent word to your godfather," he said.

I had trouble moving my tongue; I thought it must be very swollen. I made a huge effort and asked him about Enrico.

"The doctor saw him," was the only thing he told me. "Now he'll see you."

I didn't have the strength to stand, so I leaned my head back and dozed, or passed out. I opened my eyes when I felt someone touching my hand: it was a man who wore glasses, and he had a lot of freckles on his face and a blond mustache that smelled of perfume. Though it may have come from his lips. In those days there were people who perfumed their mouths.

"Don't be afraid," he whispered.

I knew he was a doctor from the way he lifted my fingers and examined the wounds.

"I'll have to take her with me," he told Nicolás Iznaga. "I can't operate here."

My tongue was a brick, one of those stones on the ground. It was painful and hard to do, but I moved the stone and said I wanted to see Enrico. The doctor looked at Nicolás Iznaga, who shook his head. I don't know where I got the strength, I think it came from my anger, but I stood up and ran to the bedroom. Nobody stopped me, and I was sure I'd find him dead. The lamp was lit, there was a very strong medicine smell, and I looked toward the bed in terror. Then I saw him, lying against some pillows, like a sea animal washed up on shore. A nun was with him, and she was bandaging his arm. He looked at me as though he was seeing a ghost.

"Aïda!"

I went to him very slowly because I couldn't see through my tears. With my good hand I stroked his face, his swollen jaw, a little cut he had next to his ear. I must have looked pretty bad too, because he raised his hand to touch me but barely brushed my skin.

"It's my fault," he said.

I didn't let him see my ruined fingers. I don't think he ever knew I lost them.

"I'm here now," was all I could think of to say.

Nicolás Iznaga came in after me and said the doctor was going to take me somewhere else to cure me, then I could come back to the house and take care of Enrico. I looked at the nun, who had finished bandaging him. She was the one who gave me courage: "Don't worry, you can go."

Enrico smiled and closed his eyes. I stared at his swollen belly, I wondered how many times he'd been punched. I looked at him and looked at him, filling my eyes as though I was filling my lungs: before going under I needed air. Nicolás Iznaga almost pulled me out of the room and almost pushed me into the hands of the doctor.

"Take her and cure her. I don't want her godfather to see her covered in blood."

We got into a car. The doctor sat beside me, and I asked him if Enrico was badly hurt.

"He is," he said. "Don't you know who hit him?"

I said I didn't know, but it seemed to me he didn't believe me. He lit a cigarette and looked down at my feet, at my shoes all covered with dirt.

"Just tell me one thing: what's Enrico Caruso doing in Trinidad?"

I closed my eyes so I wouldn't have to answer him, and he didn't say another word. We drove to the clinic, the Casa de Socorros, and a nurse put me in a bed, took off my clothes, and cleaned away the blood: it had run all down my body. I asked her if they were going to cut off my fingers, and she said I should ask the doctor. My mother told me later it was a miracle I didn't lose my arm. We didn't even think about you; nobody had any idea you were on the way. They gave me something to smell and then I didn't know anything till the next day, when the stabbing pains woke me, the pain in the fingers I didn't have anymore. A nurse brought me a cup of broth, and the doctor came in and explained what he had done to my hand. I didn't hear very much because in the middle of his explanation I saw Nicolás Iznaga, and behind him was my godfather, José de Calazán.

I felt happy and sad at the same time. Calazán came over to me, put his hand on my shoulder, and didn't open his mouth. Nicolás Iznaga was the one who spoke.

"Your mother's outside."

He hadn't finished the sentence when my mother rushed in, looked at me, and burst into tears. She was sobbing like a little girl and nobody—not the doctor, or Iznaga, or Calazán—did anything to comfort her. When she calmed down, she helped me out of bed and put a flowered dress on me and a hat she had brought from Havana. I didn't have the strength to talk, I only moved my head when they asked me something. Before we left the Casa de Socorros, the doctor showed my mother how to take care of the stitches on my hand.

"Be sure to eat well," he said to me, "and don't do anything stupid in Havana."

We got into a car that drove us to Calle del Desengaño. My mother put her arm around my shoulders, and Calazán started looking at the people, at all the life in Trinidad passing in front of our eyes. In all that time I didn't dare to ask about Enrico; I had the feeling that just asking about him could do him harm. Iznaga had gone on ahead and opened the door as soon as we got to the house. We went in and I saw that there were bundles on the floor. I knew they contained my clothes, all my things: my mother had packed everything. I looked at her and she lowered her eyes. Then I looked at Calazán.

"It's over," he said to me.

I walked very slowly to the empty bedroom. The bed wasn't made, there was still a smell of medicine. I sat on the bed and buried my face in one of the pillows. Somebody followed me and stroked my back: it was my mother.

"Aidita, listen to me, Aidita."

Without looking up I asked her when he had died.

"He didn't die," she said. "They took him back to Havana to cure him."

I shriveled inside. I didn't move for a few minutes, I was thinking. Then I stood up and walked into the living room. I looked at the bundles again: I knew the path that was waiting for me: from Disappointment in Trinidad to Bitterness in

Havana, from Calle del Desengaño to Calle Amargura. The door was open and I walked out.

Calazán came after me and grabbed my arm: "Come inside."

I had a reaction that he didn't expect: I turned like an animal and hit him in the face with my good hand; I closed my fist to hit him, so he got more than a slap, it was a punch that knocked him down. My mother ran out screaming, and behind her I saw Nicolás Iznaga, who went straight to Calazán to help him. I turned and started running, or running and falling, down the street. I crossed a square and went into a church. They were in the middle of mass, and the people turned to look at me, I was the last thing they expected to see there: a Chinese woman with the eyes of a lunatic, her hair flying, her hand wrapped in a bandage. I backed out onto the street, I didn't see anybody following me, and I walked, I didn't run, for a block or two. At the next corner something made me look up: CALLE AMARGURA was all I could see.

Until that moment I hadn't gone out of my mind. I might have looked crazy to other people, but inside, the whole time, I knew what I was doing. But that was the last straw, I became totally confused, and that street in Trinidad, because it had the same name as the one in Havana, was to blame. I forgot where I was and began to look for the Hotel Sevilla; I walked round and round in circles, asking people the way to Calle Zulueta or how to get to Trocadero. Finally, I stopped at another church, or what I thought was a church: all I saw was a high wall and the spaces where I could make out three bells.

Everything gets dark after that. I remember bits and pieces of the trip back to Havana; I remember faces, some of them familiar, others not; I even remember some dreams: I must have dreamed about Enrico every night. My mother told me I spent two months not knowing anything; I didn't remember that my name was Aida and I didn't even remember anything about my life. I was like a dead person who got up quietly every morning, ate breakfast calmly, and looked out the window. In the meantime, you were growing inside me; maybe you were sucking out all those memories, or keeping them inside you so that we could take them out one day, so that we could call them back together: that's what we've been doing all these months.

I'm not the one telling you this story, Enriqueta, because when I look into your eyes you're the one telling it to me; you're the one who brings back a gesture, a look, of your father's; you're the one who repeats Calazán's words, and Domitila's weeping, and Yuan Pei Fu's smoke. I knew you made yourself known before you came into the world: you appeared in Amable Casanova's aquamarine. She saw you and you saw us, too, from the bottom of the stone. You saw your father walking off the boat that brought him to Cuba, and later you saw him leave.

They came to Trinidad for Enrico. The impresario Adolfo Bracale came with Bruno Zirato and Mario Fantini, and the three of them persuaded him to go back to Havana, and they were only there a few hours, because the steamship *Cartago* was ready to sail.

A few weeks later my mother knew I was pregnant. She didn't tell me right away; I wouldn't have understood her anyhow. She told me she stroked my belly and whispered: "You're going to have a child, Aida," but I paid no attention. I didn't react until I was in my fourth month, one morning I woke up and said I needed cloth to sew diapers. Later on, when I was in my sixth month, a rumor went round Havana that Enrico Caruso had died in New York. That was New Year's Eve. María Vigil came by to see in the new year with us, and when the bells rang twelve times and there was shouting and noise in the street, I bowed my head and began to cry. She put her arms around me, she asked me to welcome in the year with joy.

"Don't you see, it's 1921. This is the year your baby will be born."

The newspapers said that Enrico hadn't died, though they did say he'd had an operation in a hotel in New York. They said the name of the hotel was the Vanderbilt, and without telling anybody I went to the post office and sent him a cable. I was afraid his wife would see it so I sent it to his secretary. This is what I wrote:

BRUNO ZIRATO, HOTEL VANDERBILT, NEW YORK
I BEG YOU TO TELL ENRICO HIS CHILD WILL BE BORN IN
MARCH.

I signed my complete name, Aida Petrirena Cheng, and added my address on Calle Amargura. A few weeks went by, and I lost all hope of ever getting an answer, but one morning in the middle of February there was a knock at the door and they handed my mother a cable. It came from New York, and it said that *Commendatore* Caruso was very ill, but as soon as he felt better he would be given my message. There was no name, only the initials B.Z.

I hoped you'd be born early, the same day as Enrico, February 25. But you were on time and waited for March: on the fifth, at dawn, the pains began. The rest you know: you were born a little after eleven in the morning, and your grandmother cried because she said that being a girl, you'd suffer more without your father's name. She didn't want you to be called Enriqueta, but I insisted, I still had the hope of seeing Enrico again.

When you were almost three months old, I took you to the house on Calle Manrique. I went there every once in a while so that Yuan Pei Fu could see you, after all, he was your real grandfather. I saw the papers at a newsstand. I was holding you in my arms, and a woman buying some magazines stopped to look at you. "What a cute little Chinese doll," she said, though you weren't Chinese. I didn't have time to answer her, because one of the papers had something about your father, I went closer and this is what I read: "Great send-off for Caruso in New York. Tenor to spend summer in Naples." I practically dropped you, my legs turned to rubber, and I almost asked somebody to help me. I knew Enrico was going straight to his death and from now on I shouldn't hope for anything.

At about this time, Calazán came to Havana to see you. Things between us had been straightened out: a godfather can never break with his goddaughter, and his goddaughter can't break with him even if she wants to. He gave you a protection as a gift, and asked me to bring you to Regla in the beginning of August. I asked him why it had to be then. He took you in his arms, he made the sign of the cross over you with his rough fingers, and he put you back in your cradle.

"I have to help her say goodbye to her father."

On the night of August first you were very restless. You moaned in your sleep and kept waking up and crying. That's how you were until about two in the morning, when you finally fell into a more peaceful sleep. I began to walk around the house in the dark, my mother got up and came to keep me company, she said she couldn't sleep either and was thinking about my grandmother. We heated up some coffee and drank it sitting by the window and looking out at the empty street. I asked her why she had picked a street with such a sad name to live on. She said she hadn't picked anything: Noro Cheng had taken her there to live when they got married because it was the house Yuan Pei Fu bought for them. It was the first time she ever talked to me about the strange arrangement between one Chinaman who had loved her and another who did no more than live with her.

We stopped talking because we heard footsteps. The footsteps sounded very loud on the paving stones, and we both had the same impulse and looked toward the place where the sound was coming from. My mother leaned out, trying to see who was walking at that hour. "A man's coming this way," she said. I leaned out, too, and saw the figure with a hat and cane, a blurred figure moving very fast. Suddenly the sound of footsteps stopped. We saw the man but didn't hear him walking. I was confused and turned to my mother, who glanced away from the street to look at me. It was just for a second, but when we looked out again the man had disappeared, and as soon as he disappeared the sound of his footsteps started up again, footsteps but no body, and they seemed to stop at the door of our house.

"It's Enrico," I said to my mother.

"It's nobody," she answered, but she was trembling.

You woke up and began to cry. It wasn't a hunger cry, or a cry to be picked up. It was another kind of cry that we couldn't understand, as though something hurt you inside. You were only five months old, but you were crying like a grown person.

Two days later the papers reported the news: Enrico Caruso had died in Naples, at seven past nine in the morning, and with the difference in time, that was the moment we saw the figure walking, the figure of a man who disappeared on the street. I went into mourning and cried all that day and the day after that. Then I stopped crying, and little by little I found comfort in you.

When I took you to Calazán, on the sixth or seventh of August, just as he had told me to, I asked him the meaning of the footsteps we heard that night. My godfather said that when somebody dies with unfinished business, a messenger from his soul leaves the place of his death and flies to the place of his destiny. The place of his final destiny was my house. It had always been my house. Souls have a certain number of journeys, and this messenger had come to see you, Enriqueta, to say goodbye to the two of us, in sorrow and in love.

My godfather took you in his arms and asked for the gold nugget Enrico had given me, the memento of the bomb that I've kept for you, because it has that splinter, a sliver of wood shaken loose by the explosion. He passed the piece of gold along your arms, he passed it over your head and made the sign of a cross with it: "Say goodbye to your father, girl," he said two or three times, and you started to laugh. Then he wrapped the nugget in a red cloth and gave it back to me.

"The man was a child of Changó," he said. "But now you see that water puts out the flame."

I didn't dare tell him that he was wrong. That his flame was with us, burning in you and me, burning in Regla, in the Lagoon of San Joaquín, in Santa Clara, and burning most of all in Trinidad, those places where we loved each other so much.

I came back to this house with you, and you grew up, you became the woman you are now. I've told you the story knowing that deep down you already knew it. I've only pulled one thread, pulled it out of your soul. Your memories and mine came together and walked together all these months, and today the story is finished, it ends here, with me.

Let's finish it once and for all. Come closer, Enriqueta, and give me a kiss. Let's write the words together. *The End.*

*T*wenty days later, on the sixth of December, 1952, while I was helping her to sit up in bed, my mother collapsed in my arms. She never regained consciousness and died the next day, late in the morning. The same neighbor who had helped me take care of her asked me to leave the room, and she combed and dressed her. María Vigil showed up a little while later and took charge of arrangements for the wake.

They were difficult days for me, getting used to her absence and putting the pages of her story in order. At times I asked myself why I had taken on the task of writing it down, and then I would conclude that these papers would be of some use to me later. Perhaps my children would read them, if I ever brought any children into the world.

On Christmas Eve of that same year, a colleague of mine at the Blue Network invited me to supper at her house. At first I thanked her but said my mother's death was too recent. Then I changed my mind and went to have supper with her and her entire family. A friend of her husband's had also been invited. I recognized him as soon as we shook hands: it was Israel Trujillo, the watchmaker I had met some months before at the house of his brother Abadelio, the music critic for the Diario de la Marina.

Israel still lived in Güines, and that night he spoke to me about his widowhood and his profession. My colleague insisted I come back to celebrate the new year, but I said it had always been a very special date for my mother, and I preferred to spend it on Calle Amargura. But I did accept an invitation from Israel to have lunch on New Year's Day. He wasn't a very young man, or especially attractive, but I believe we understood something important that night: for good or ill, we were basically alike. We were both very passive, and we suffered from the same timidity, the same distrust of our emotions. Neither of us had the capacity to be carried away by anything or anybody, the ability that others have to give themselves over to hope, to lose their heads.

After lunch on the first of January, we discovered that we also shared an unusual fondness for going to movies in Chinatown and watching paisano films. In my case it was understandable, since I was the granddaughter of a Cantonese. But in Israel the taste for those tales, some of them sung and others not, did not seem justified.

Even so, on weekends we went to the Golden Eagle—that was the name of one theater—or to the New Continental, the name of the other. Both of them smelled of damp, some of the Chinese would spit on the floor, many of them would cough, and they clapped when a famous singer appeared on the screen or when a battle scene ended. It was in one of those movie houses, during an intermission, that I told Israel I was planning a trip to Cienfuegos. He didn't say anything right away, but later on, after we left the movie, he asked what day I planned to go and how long I intended to stay. I said I would leave that week and not stay more than three or four days, just the time I needed to locate a physician, Dr. Benito Terry, and talk to him about my mother. Israel said he had an idea: when I came back, if it was all right with me, we could be married.

Until that moment we had kissed only once, on the previous Sunday, in the darkness of the New Continental. That afternoon, as we said goodbye at the door to my house, we kissed again, we embraced, and Israel showed more passion than he had on other occasions, and wished me a good trip.

I went to Cienfuegos by bus. Since the ride was so long, I had time to think about my solitude, about marriage, about what my life would be like with Israel. I had been engaged to be married twice: the first time, when I was twenty, to my first boyfriend, an employee at the Sarrá Pharmacy, the biggest pharmacy in Havana. The second time, when I was twenty-five, to a traveling salesman I met at a dance. My first engagement was ended by the boy's mother:

he was a white boy who took classes at night, and in those days it was considered scandalous to marry a woman whose father was not known, who had a Chinese name from her mother and mulatta blood from her grandmother.

My plans with the traveling salesman went a little further: we set a date, my mother insisted it be in June. But he changed his mind just a few months before the wedding. He realized that an enterprising, adventurous man did not have much in common with a retiring woman who almost never responded in kind to his ardor and his advances, not because she was chaste or ignorant but because she had a different understanding of affection, or because of some unchanging trait in her character. I've said it before: my mother and father were so passionately in love that perhaps, when I was conceived, they left me a little hollow, distant with men, or fearful, perhaps. Traveling on the bus, I could accept, for the first time, what I hadn't wanted to accept before: the traveling salesman had become disenchanted. He had grown tired of me, and what was worse, I had never met the person who could make me want to leave everything, risk everything, for his sake, and at this stage of my life, when I was almost thirty-two, I probably never would.

When I arrived in Cienfuegos I went directly to the Hotel Gran Prado, asked for a room, and went up to change. Later, with the help of a hotel employee who provided me with a list of physicians, I found Benito Terry's telephone number. I called that same day, and a woman answered. I lied to her, saying I was a former patient who had come all the way from Havana to consult with the doctor.

"The doctor is retired," she said. "He isn't well."

I insisted, I pleaded, I tried to soften her with the argument that my mother's life depended on it. And it was true, to an extent, even though my mother had died. She hesitated, then left the phone to speak to the doctor. After a few minutes she returned and said the doctor would see me the next day, at ten in the morning. She gave me the address and told me to be punctual.

That night I ate alone in a restaurant near the hotel. After supper I went for a walk. I began on the Calzada de Dolores, where my mother had lived for a short time. I didn't know the exact address of the house, so I looked at all the houses with great interest, searching for some trace, an aura, a presentiment. It was after nine, but I stopped a taxi and told the driver to take me to Calle Urrutiner. He asked where along that street, and I told him I wanted to know if a store called La Bandera Americana was still there. He smiled and said it was, but at this time of night it would be closed. I asked him to take me there anyway, and when I saw the sign I felt a very sweet sorrow run through me, a kind of nostalgia at knowing this was where my mother had bought the fan I buried with her. I got out and looked through the glass. It was all I could do: make an effort to find a shop window, the one that broke my heart, the one that displayed fans that were waiting, because they really seemed to be waiting for something.

I went back to the cab and asked the driver to go on to the Teatro Tomás Terry. I saw it at night, shrouded in a strange light, and I think it was better to see it this way, distant and mysterious, as if it were still submerged in the waters of time, in the afternoon when Caruso came there to rehearse and a violinist stood up to die.

The following morning I dressed very carefully for my visit with Benito Terry. I didn't want him to think I was just some woman begging for old gossip. I wasn't sure if I ought to tell him the truth or invent a story, as I had already done so many times. The woman who had answered the phone came to the door and asked me in. She was dressed in a nurse's uniform, and except for her, I didn't see another person in the house. We walked down a hallway lined with earthenware jars and came to a rectangular courtyard that seemed like a hall of mirrors: ivy-covered arches looked across at one another, and the statues, four on each side, were placed at identical intervals. Even the rocking chairs faced each other and gave the same *impression of a reflected image. A man sat rocking gently in one of the chairs, disturbing the mirror, or the mid-morning illusion: Benito Terry was still blond, very old but blond, and his mustache and beard were thick. Later I learned he no longer used scent.*

"I understand your mother has sent you to see me," he said after we had exchanged greetings.

My legs trembled as if I had been discovered committing a crime. Benito Terry was blind: he leaned on a cane while he spoke to me, and he moved his eyes back and forth in that anguished way of people move them who are still not resigned to the darkness.

"She's the woman whose fingers you amputated more than thirty years ago. It was in Trinidad; do you remember her?"

He did not answer. He tilted his head to one side and remained in that position for a long time, immobile, not saying a word. I was afraid he had fainted. I didn't dare say anything else but tried to catch sight of the nurse, who had disappeared after leaving me there.

"Aida Cheng," he murmured at last, when I was about to call for help. "She lost three fingers and had a nervous breakdown. The last time I saw her, she was sitting in front of the Popa del Barco Hermitage, crying for Enrico Caruso."

"That's why I'm here," I told him. "I want to know what happened."

Benito Terry lifted his cane and moved it forward, as if he were showing me a path.

"Why don't you go and ask her?"

"She died two months ago," I said, playing the card I considered the final one, the only one possible.

"She died," Benito Terry whispered, "and Caruso died a long time ago of the beating they gave him. But I'm still here, suffering my misfortune, the misfortune that befell me in Trinidad de Cuba because of those two."

The nurse returned with a glass of milk for him and a little tray with two or three pills on it. She glanced at me without much cordiality and asked if I wanted something to drink.

"Bring her a cognac," the doctor told her. "Her mother died."

He tossed the pills in his mouth and then took a sip of milk. Only one, and handed the glass back to the nurse.

They came for me here, in this very house. The man who came for me was Nicolás Iznaga, who had a Congo brotherhood somewhere in Palmira. He was a respectable black man, he showed up here at six in the morning and said he needed me to see someone who was gravely injured in Trinidad, a very important man. My wife begged me not to go; she had gotten it into her head that it was some fight between brotherhoods, that the wounded man was surely some brujo, a ñáñigo who had been stabbed. I was used to going to Trinidad to treat wealthy people who had fallen off horses or had been injured in some way. I took the boat with Iznaga and reached Trinidad about noon. We came in on Casilda and from there we went straight to Calle Desengaño, to an absolutely ordinary house. There I found the last thing I expected to see: Enrico Caruso, being tended to by a couple of black women, lying in an unmade bed and covered with blood. I was young and very impressionable, and I wanted to take him to the Casa de Socorros, but they wouldn't allow it. Caruso himself didn't want to be moved. He said he was waiting for his secretary, who would be there soon.

The fact was that he had been beaten. He had a fractured rib. Six months later it had to be removed in an improvised operating room at the Hotel Vanderbilt in New York. The doctors were at their wits' end, abscesses were beginning to form near Caruso's kidneys and all around his chest, and none of them thought to ask if he had been hit. He said nothing, of course, about what had happened in Trinidad; his secretary didn't mention it, and I certainly didn't

*have the courage to say anything. The man was doomed from the
time he left Cuba. It was a matter of months; I don't believe he
lasted a year.*

He stopped to clear his throat, and at that moment the nurse came
back with a cognac I didn't want. I accepted it out of courtesy and
waited for her to leave so I could spill it out. But Benito Terry, blind as
he was, guessed my intentions and told me to give him the glass.

"The doctors were to blame," he continued, after drinking the
cognac down in one swallow.

*Especially the ones in the United States. Puccini himself—do you
know who Puccini was?—wrote a letter to a friend of his, a woman
who had been very ill. I have a copy of the letter, it was published in
a New York newspaper. He said something like this: "Poor Caruso,
what a sad fate. . . . While an Italian doctor is saving you, the
Americans are killing Caruso."*

*In reality, Caruso died of peritonitis, of septicemia. Listen care-
fully: he rotted from the inside. There were five or six Italian doctors
in the hotel room in Naples where he died. What do you think they
saw? The same thing I saw when I left him there in Trinidad: a poor
soul whose body had failed him. In his final hours he was paralyzed,
he couldn't even drink, though he was dying of thirst. Only his
throat was alive. He kept speaking out of that throat, though no one
could explain what he might have talked about while he was dying.*

*Many articles were written afterward. They all asked the same
thing: What did he die of? What did he die of? There was an Italian
professor, a man named Chiarolanza or Carolanza, who looked into
a few things. He wrote an article; I keep it with my papers. He said
there were factors that could not be explained in the death of
Caruso, mistakes in the treatment he received, followed by what he
called "incomprehensible fatalism." And that was the conclusion he*

reached: for those who believe in destiny, things happened as they had to happen. Caruso couldn't escape the libretto, he couldn't skip a line. Fatality is the only opera we never have to study: we're born knowing it by heart.

Your mother, the woman whose fingers I amputated, was a fatalist. That day, when I found her in front of the Popa del Barco Hermitage, this is what she said to me: "If they take him to Naples, Enrico will die." I had a message for her, a message that Caruso had left for her before he went to Havana. But I realized she was very disoriented, almost out of her mind, and it didn't seem to me as if she was in any condition to receive messages. On the previous afternoon, at the Casa de Socorros, I had treated her wounds, cleaned off the blood: her whole body was covered in dried blood. The same men who had beaten Caruso had beaten her. I think they made off with her because they thought she was a famous singer, and when they discovered she wasn't, they decided to leave her in Caniquí, that cave at the bottom of La Vigía. Her good fortune was that the Congos are like rats: they know every hiding place, and they help one another. When they told Nicolás Iznaga what had happened, he acted with great intelligence: first he came for me, took me to Enrico Caruso, and left me to care for him while he went with his band of Congos to find Aida.

They brought her back at two or three in the afternoon. She had bled half to death and was starving, and even so the only thing that woman asked for was to see Caruso. Iznaga wanted to put an end to that madness, and he told her she couldn't. And suddenly I saw her get up and run; she was in his room in a flash, I didn't think she could even stand, let alone run like that. She was with Caruso for a while, but he kept dozing off because of the sedative I had given him. Then Iznaga dragged her out by force, and had to hand her over to me by force. He asked me to take care of her, to sew back those fingers or cut them off once and for all, anything so that her family wouldn't see her in that condition.

While she was sleeping at the Casa de Socorros, they came for Caruso. Three men, all Italian, they showed up very discreetly in Trinidad and gave out money left and right. The impresario Bracale was one of them; he talked almost like a Cuban, and he pleaded with me not to say anything about what had happened. I promised him I wouldn't, and he tried to pay me an exorbitant amount of money for the little I had been able to do in that house, with no means to determine exactly what Caruso's condition was internally. I refused the money, of course, and reminded him that he was speaking to a gentleman, a Terry, in fact.

When it was time to go, Caruso seemed improved; at least he could stand. Before he got into the car he took me aside and asked what had happened to Aida. I told him the truth: that I had been obliged to amputate some fingers, but that she was young and strong and would soon recover. That's when he gave me the message for her, he made me swear I wouldn't give it to anyone else.

But you already know that your mother attempted to escape. When she returned to the house and didn't see the tenor, she began to run through the town and went into Santísima Trinidad, interrupted the mass, had a nervous attack, and finally ended up at the hermitage. Tell me what message I could have given her there, in the middle of the street, surrounded by all those Congos who had come for her, and in front of that woman, Aida's mother, that is to say, your grandmother, a hysterical mulatta who kept screaming Aida, Aida, Aida.

There's a belief among the natives on one of the Pacific islands, I think it is, I read it somewhere when I was a boy with no worries, a rich kid from Cienfuegos, an absolute imbecile. . . . Well, in any event, according to this belief there is a kind of misfortune that sometimes falls like an open blanket over certain people, and each of them gets a piece of the blanket—in other words, a piece of the misfortune. The affliction may differ from one person to the next, but only in *appearance, because at bottom there are threads that join them, stitches that connect them, the same cloth that simply changes color.*

One of those blankets fell over us at a certain moment in our lives. It doesn't matter that your mother was in Havana and Caruso was in New York and I was here, my career all arranged, on my way to becoming a famous doctor, married to a wonderful woman, with a future that no one could have predicted would darken so tragically. Your mother, poor woman, I don't know what kind of life she had. But look at Caruso; he had none at all because he died. And look at me: I returned to Cienfuegos, I took to my bed, and nothing mattered to me anymore. I didn't care about my wife, or the child she was expecting; today he's a doctor, but he lives in Havana. And I didn't care at all about my career. The misfortune that befell me was the worst of all, because it had no justification. In my day it was called melancholia. I was sick with sadness, emptiness, a profound disillusionment, and my wife, who hadn't wanted me to go to Trinidad that morning, died with the conviction that I had intervened in a dispute between brotherhoods, that I had treated a brujo, a ñáñigo, and that treating him had made me sick.

I don't know why I didn't tell her I had been tending Enrico Caruso. Perhaps because at first I didn't think she would believe me. And when I came back from Trinidad I was so exhausted, so sick of everything, that even the possibility of opening my mouth to explain anything made me tired. A few years later, before she died, I told her. I said that nothing unusual had happened in Trinidad. That if I had changed, if my character and my life had become a catastrophe after that day, it was sheer coincidence, the catastrophe would have happened in any event, even if I had never left Cienfuegos.

She didn't believe me. I've told you she died convinced I had been the victim of a spell, of witchcraft. And then I recalled what I had read about the blanket of misfortune that falls and is shared. In the eyes of Caruso, that great man, I saw something that frightened me. I saw it, too, in the eyes of your mother, Chinese eyes that happened to be very beautiful. Dirty and disheveled as she was, I remember your mother as an impressive woman.

But not even that could keep me from seeing what was deep inside. Death always wins, and grieving doesn't do much good. In Trinidad that day I saw a pit of oil, a black abyss, absolute nothingness. As if there had been an explosion, and behind the smoke I had been left blank. I was in bed for a long time, I would cry at night, especially at dawn. Then I stopped crying, I lived my life with a coldness that hurt others: my wife, my son, even my patients. I turned into a machine, or a vegetable. My wife couldn't bear it, and she died young. And I, because I had so little interest in anything, I lost my sight. So you see, compared to your mother or Caruso, my life was the worst of all.

Then he fell silent. It was an unendurable silence, something viscous, resembling vertigo. I recalled the image of the pit of oil and was afraid that Benito Terry would drag me after him into a void.

"I'm going to ask one thing," I said as I stood up. "I'm going to ask you to tell me the message that Caruso left for my mother."

Benito Terry gave off a withered smell, he leaned on his cane, and he stood up too. It was a great effort for his bones, and perhaps an effort for his memory: I had the impression his body no longer remembered what to do in order to stand or walk.

"It was a very obscure message. I never could understand it."

"Maybe I'll understand it," I said. The atmosphere in the courtyard was choking me. I began to perspire and thought of how my father perspired.

"Come to think of it," said Benito Terry, "that message is probably the thing that ruined my life."

He took a little bell from his pocket and rang without stopping until the nurse appeared.

"This lady is leaving now," he told her. "Walk her to the door."

* * *

A week after I returned to Havana, I married Israel Trujillo. We repaired this house on Calle Amargura and always lived here, and he opened a small watchmaking shop on Calle Galiano. It was very well known, and people would bring in their valuable watches. In 1961 the government nationalized the shop, but they asked him if he wanted to stay on as an employee. He agreed, though the salary was small, because in his heart the only thing he cared about was repairing watches. He didn't leave the shop until the middle of 1968; that was the year he got sick. Just like my mother, Israel died of cancer, and I cried for him more than I had ever cried for anyone.

At the time, his brother Abadelio was a frail old man, and times were so hard and so many things were scarce that he depended on us for everything. And so when Israel died I proposed that he come to live with me, and he was happy to accept, because he had always been fond of me.

We lived together peacefully for many years, until he also passed away. Abadelio brought his record player with him, and at night we would listen to opera, we'd play records by Enrico Caruso, and I took great pleasure in my father's voice; it made me sad not to have known him.

Israel never believed I was Caruso's natural child. He had accepted this story of mine as if it were a whim, a mania, one of those defects people have, but not one that hides their other virtues. His brother Abadelio, on the other hand, believed every word of my story, and at night, after we had eaten, he would pick up a record in each hand, wave them both around, and say:

"Let's listen to your father. Which do you prefer: 'Oh, mostruosa colpa' or 'M'apparì tutt'amor'?"

He knew very well I preferred 'M'apparì tutt'amor.' I knew it by heart and would sing it under my breath, my eyes not focused on anything, as if I were singing to a ghost.

*   *   *

On June 13, 1970, I went to the radio station as usual. By this time the Blue Network had disappeared and I was working in the newsroom at Radio Progreso. An announcer named Aurelio Suárez and I took turns reading the news: I would read one news report and he would read the next, and when they were very long, we would divide up the paragraphs. That day, after announcing the headlines, it was my turn to read this note:

Today is the fiftieth anniversary of the explosion at the Teatro Nacional, when the tenor Enrico Caruso ran through the streets of Havana dressed in the picturesque costume of the warrior Radamès. Where did the great singer take refuge? In the Parque Central, as some said? In the kitchen of the Hotel Inglaterra, as others claimed? Or is it true that he climbed into the first car he saw and locked himself in the Hotel Sevilla for several days?

Then it was Aurelio's turn to read:

There was a comic note in the flight of Radamès and Amonasro. Radamès, following "Ritorna vincitor," had to run defenseless onto Calle Consulado. To a watchman who offered to protect him, the great singer had to say the sacramental phrase: "Vigilante io resto a te." A short time later Amonasro appeared: gasping for breath, sweating, half naked in his tigerskin and the wild boar tusks around his neck. In friendship he proposed to Radamès that they "fugir'" to the hotel. And Caruso willingly agreed. It was the first time in Aïda that Radamès was saved from the "fatal pietra" by a fatal bomb.

Inexorably, the last paragraph had been marked for me to read: "Today, June 13, fifty years after the event that stirred all of Havana, the mystery persists."

When we finished, Aurelio began to gather up his papers. He put his ballpoint pen back in his pocket, and since he was a good-natured sort, he came out with this remark:

"Damn! That Caruso was really something."

I looked up, I still don't know what made me say it.

"Caruso was my father, and it's fifty years ago today that he met my mother."

Aurelio stopped short and looked at me in astonishment because he knew I wasn't a woman who made jokes.

"Isn't your name Enriqueta Cheng?"

"That's my mother's name," I said. "But I'm Caruso's daughter."

He was very serious for a few seconds, very few, actually. Then he shook his head and burst out laughing.

"Don't try to kid me, Enriqueta. If you're Caruso's daughter, then I'm the son of the Knight Errant of Paris."

He was referring to a famous beggar who wandered the streets of Havana. I started to laugh too, and together we walked out of the studio.

It was the last time I ever said I was my father's daughter.